THE BROWNIES

AND OTHER TALES

JULIANA HORATIA EWING

1ST WORLD
LIBRARY
Literary Society

The Brownies and Other Tales

Juliana Horatia Ewing

© 1st World Library, 2009
PO Box 2211
Fairfield, IA 52556
www.1stworldlibrary.com
First Edition

LCCN: 2009923470

Softcover ISBN: 978-1-4218-8859-0
Hardcover ISBN: 978-1-4218-8958-0
eBook ISBN: 978-1-4218-8760-9

Purchase *"The Brownies and Other Tales"*
as a traditional bound book at:
www.1stWorldLibrary.com/purchase.asp?ISBN=978-1-4218-8859-0

1st World Library is a literary, educational organization
dedicated to:

- Creating a free internet library of downloadable ebooks

- Hosting writing competitions and offering book publishing
scholarships.

Interested in more 1st World Library books? contact:
literacy@1stworldlibrary.com
Check us out at: www.1stworldlibrary.com

1ˢᵗ World Library Literary Society

Giving Back to the World

"If you want to work on the core problem, it's early school literacy."

- James Barksdale, former CEO of Netscape

"No skill is more crucial to the future of a child, or to a democratic and prosperous society, than literacy."

- Los Angeles Times

"Literacy... means far more than learning how to read and write... The aim is to transmit... knowledge and promote social participation."

- UNESCO

"Literacy is not a luxury, it is a right and a responsibility. If our world is to meet the challenges of the twenty-first century we must harness the energy and creativity of all our citizens."

- President Bill Clinton

"Parents should be encouraged to read to their children, and teachers should be equipped with all available techniques for teaching literacy, so the varying needs and capacities of individual kids can be taken into account."

- Hugh Mackay

DEDICATED

TO

MY VERY DEAR AND HONOURED MOTHER

J.H.E.

1871

CONTENTS

THE BROWNIES

A little girl sat sewing and crying on a garden seat. She had fair floating hair, which the breeze blew into her eyes, and between the cloud of hair, and the mist of tears, she could not see her work very clearly. She neither tied up her locks, nor dried her eyes, however; for when one is miserable, one may as well be completely so.

"What is the matter?" said the Doctor, who was a friend of the Rector's, and came into the garden whenever he pleased.

The Doctor was a tall stout man, with hair as black as crow's feathers on the top, and grey underneath, and a bushy beard. When young, he had been slim and handsome, with wonderful eyes, which were wonderful still; but that was many years past. He had a great love for children, and this one was a particular friend of his.

"What is the matter?" said he.

"I'm in a row," murmured the young lady through her veil; and the needle went in damp, and came out with a jerk, which is apt to result in what ladies called "puckering."

"You are like London in a yellow fog," said the Doctor, throwing himself on to the grass, "and it is very depressing to my feelings. What is the row about, and how came you to get into it?"

"We're all in it," was the reply; and apparently the fog was thickening, for the voice grew less and less distinct—"the boys and everybody. It's all about forgetting, and not putting away, and leaving about, and borrowing, and breaking, and that sort of thing. I've had Father's new pocket-handkerchiefs to hem, and I've been out climbing with the boys, and kept forgetting and forgetting, and Mother says I always forget; and I can't help it. I forget to tidy his newspapers for him, and I forget to feed Puss, and I forgot these; besides, they're a great bore, and Mother gave them to Nurse to do, and this one was lost, and we found it this morning tossing about in the toy-cupboard."

"It looks as if it had been taking violent exercise," said the Doctor. "But what have the boys to do with it?"

"Why, then there was a regular turn out of the toys," she explained, "and they're all in a regular mess. You know, we always go on till the last minute, and then things get crammed in anyhow. Mary and I did tidy them once or twice; but the boys never put anything away, you know, so what's the good?"

"What, indeed!" said the Doctor. "And so you have complained of them?"

"Oh! no!" answered she. "We don't get them into rows, unless they are very provoking; but some of the things were theirs, so everybody was sent for, and I was sent out to finish this, and they are all tidying. I don't know when it will be done, for I have all this side to hem; and the soldiers' box is broken, and Noah is lost out of the Noah's Ark, and so is one of the elephants and a guinea-pig, and so is the rocking-horse's nose;

and nobody knows what has become of Rutlandshire and the Wash, but they're so small, I don't wonder; only North America and Europe are gone too."

The Doctor started up in affected horror. "Europe gone, did you say? Bless me! what will become of us!"

"Don't!" said the young lady, kicking petulantly with her dangling feet, and trying not to laugh. "You know I mean the puzzles; and if they were yours, you wouldn't like it."

"I don't half like it as it is," said the Doctor. "I am seriously alarmed. An earthquake is one thing; you have a good shaking, and settle down again. But Europe gone—lost—Why, here comes Deordie, I declare, looking much more cheerful than we do; let us humbly hope that Europe has been found. At present I feel like Aladdin when his palace had been transported by the magician; I don't know where I am."

"You're here, Doctor; aren't you?" asked the slow curly-wigged brother, squatting himself on the grass.

"*Is* Europe found?" said the Doctor tragically.

"Yes," laughed Deordie. "I found it."

"You will be a great man," said the Doctor. "And—it is only common charity to ask—how about North America?"

"Found too," said Deordie. "But the Wash is completely lost."

"And my six shirts in it!" said the Doctor. "I sent them last Saturday as ever was. What a world we live in! Any more news? Poor Tiny here has been crying her eyes out."

"I'm so sorry, Tiny," said the brother. "But don't bother about it. It's all square now, and we're going to have a new shelf put up."

"Have you found everything?" asked Tiny.

"Well, not the Wash, you know. And the elephant and the guinea-pig are gone for good; so the other elephant and the other guinea-pig must walk together as a pair now. Noah was among the soldiers, and we have put the cavalry into a night-light box. Europe and North America were behind the book-case; and, would you believe it? the rocking-horse's nose has turned up in the nursery oven."

"I can't believe it," said the Doctor. "The rocking-horse's nose couldn't turn up, it was the purest Grecian, modelled from the Elgin marbles. Perhaps it was the heat that did it, though. However, you seem to have got through your troubles very well, Master Deordie. I wish poor Tiny were at the end of her task."

"So do I," said Deordie ruefully. "But I tell you what I've been thinking, Doctor. Nurse is always nagging at us, and we're always in rows of one sort or another, for doing this, and not doing that, and leaving our things about. But, you know, it's a horrid shame, for there are plenty of servants, and I don't see why we should be always bothering to do little things, and—"

"Oh! come to the point, please," said the Doctor; "you do go round the square so, in telling your stories, Deordie. What have you been thinking of?"

"Well," said Deordie, who was as good-tempered as he was slow, "the other day Nurse shut me up in the back nursery for borrowing her scissors and losing them; but I'd got 'Grimm' inside one of my knickerbockers, so when she locked the door, I sat down to read. And I read the story of the Shoe-maker and the little Elves who came and did his work for him before he got up; and I thought it would be so jolly if we had some little Elves to do things instead of us."

"That's what Tommy Trout said," observed the Doctor.

"Who's Tommy Trout?" asked Deordie.

"Don't you know, Deor?" said Tiny. "It's the good boy who pulled the cat out of the what's-his-name.

'Who pulled her out?
Little Tommy Trout.'

Is it the same Tommy Trout, Doctor? I never heard anything else about him except his pulling the cat out; and I can't think how he did that."

"Let down the bucket for her, of course," said the Doctor. "But listen to me. If you will get that handkerchief done, and take it to your mother with a kiss, and not keep me waiting, I'll have you all to tea, and tell you the story of Tommy Trout."

"This very night?" shouted Deordie.

"This very night."

"Every one of us?" inquired the young gentleman with rapturous incredulity.

"Every one of you.—Now, Tiny, how about that work?"

"It's just done," said Tiny.—"Oh! Deordie, climb up behind,

and hold back my hair, there's a darling, while I fasten off. Oh! Deor, you're pulling my hair out. Don't."

"I want to make a pig-tail," said Deor.

"You can't," said Tiny, with feminine contempt. "You can't plait. What's the good of asking boys to do anything? There! it's done at last. Now go and ask Mother if we may go. Will you let me come, Doctor," she inquired, "if I do as you said?"

"To be sure I will," he answered. "Let me look at you. Your eyes are swollen with crying. How can you be such a silly little goose?"

"Did you never cry?" asked Tiny.

"When I was your age? Well, perhaps so."

"You've never cried since, surely," said Tiny.

The Doctor absolutely blushed.

"What do you think?" said he.

"Oh, of course not," she answered. "You've nothing to cry about. You're grown up, and you live all alone in a beautiful house, and you do as you like, and never get into rows, or have anybody but yourself to think about; and no nasty pocket-handkerchiefs to hem."

"Very nice; eh, Deordie?" said the Doctor.

"Awfully jolly," said Deordie.

"Nothing else to wish for, eh?"

Juliana Horatia Ewing

"*I* should keep harriers, and not a poodle, if I were a man," said Deordie; "but I suppose you could, if you wanted to."

"Nothing to cry about, at any rate?"

"I should think not!" said Deordie.—"There's Mother, though; let's go and ask her about the tea;" and off they ran.

The Doctor stretched his six feet of length upon the sward, dropped his grey head on a little heap of newly-mown grass, and looked up into the sky.

"Awfully jolly—no nasty pocket-handkerchiefs to hem," said he, laughing to himself. "Nothing else to wish for; nothing to cry about."

Nevertheless, he lay still, staring at the sky, till the smile died away, and tears came into his eyes. Fortunately, no one was there to see.

What could this "awfully jolly" Doctor be thinking of to make him cry? He was thinking of a grave-stone in the churchyard close by, and of a story connected with this grave-stone which was known to everybody in the place who was old enough to remember it. This story has nothing to do with the present story, so it ought not to be told.

And yet it has to do with the Doctor, and is very short, so it shall be put in, after all.

THE STORY OF A GRAVE-STONE

One early spring morning, about twenty years before, a man going to his work at sunrise through the churchyard, stopped by a flat stone which he had lately helped to lay down. The day before, a name had been cut on it, which he stayed to read; and below the name some one had scrawled a few words in pencil, which he read also—*Pitifully behold the sorrows of our hearts*. On the stone lay a pencil, and a few feet from it lay the Doctor, face downwards, as he had lain all night, with the hoar frost on his black hair.

Ah! these grave-stones (they were ugly things in those days; not the light, hopeful, pretty crosses we set up now), how they seem remorselessly to imprison and keep our dear dead friends away from us! And yet they do not lie with a feather's weight upon the souls that are gone, while GOD only knows how heavily they press upon the souls that are left behind. Did the spirit whose body was with the dead, stand that morning by the body whose spirit was with the dead, and pity him? Let us only talk about what we know.

After this it was said that the Doctor had got a fever, and was dying, but he got better of it; and then that he was out of his mind, but he got better of that, and came out looking much as usual, except that his hair never seemed quite so black again, as if a little of that night's hoar frost still remained. And no further misfortune happened to him that I ever heard of; and as time went on he grew a beard, and got stout, and kept a German poodle, and gave tea-parties to other people's children. As to the grave-stone story, whatever it was to him at the end of twenty years, it was a great convenience to his friends; for when he said anything they didn't agree with, or did anything they couldn't understand, or didn't say or do what was expected of him, what could be easier or more conclusive than to shake one's head and say,

"The fact is, our Doctor has been a little odd, *ever since*—!"

THE DOCTOR'S TEA-PARTY

There is one great advantage attendant upon invitations to tea with a doctor. No objections can be raised on the score of health. It is obvious that it must be fine enough to go out when the Doctor asks you, and that his tea-cakes may be eaten with perfect impunity.

Those tea-cakes were always good; to-night they were utterly delicious; there was a perfect *abandon* of currants, and the amount of citron peel was enervating to behold. Then the housekeeper waited in awful splendour, and yet the Doctor's authority over her seemed as absolute as if he were an Eastern despot. Deordie must be excused for believing in the charms of living alone. It certainly has its advantages. The limited sphere of duty conduces to discipline in the household, demand does not exceed supply in the article of waiting, and there is not that general scrimmage of conflicting interests which besets a large family in the most favoured circumstances. The housekeeper waits in black silk, and looks as if she had no meaner occupation than to sit in a rocking-chair, and dream of damson cheese.

Rustling, hospitable, and subservient, this one retired at last, and—

"Now," said the Doctor, "for the verandah; and to look at the moon."

The company adjourned with a rush, the rear being brought up by the poodle, who seemed quite used to the proceedings; and there under the verandah, framed with passion-flowers and geraniums, the Doctor had gathered mats, rugs, cushions, and arm-chairs, for the party; while far up in the sky, a yellow-faced harvest moon looked down in awful benignity.

"Now!" said the Doctor. "Take your seats. Ladies first, and gentlemen afterwards. Mary and Tiny, race for the American rocking-chair. Well done! Of course it will hold both. Now, boys, shake down. No one is to sit on the stone, or put his feet on the grass: and when you're ready, I'll begin."

"We're ready," said the girls.

The boys shook down in a few minutes more, and the Doctor began the story of

"THE BROWNIES."

"Bairns are a burden," said the Tailor to himself as he sat at work. He lived in a village on some of the glorious moors of the north of England; and by bairns he meant children, as every Northman knows.

"Bairns are a burden," and he sighed.

"Bairns are a blessing," said the old lady in the window. "It is the family motto. The Trouts have had large families and good luck for generations; that is, till your grandfather's time. He had one only son. I married him. He was a good husband, but he had been a spoilt child. He had always been used to be waited upon, and he couldn't fash to look after the farm when it was his own. We had six children. They are all dead but you, who were the youngest. You were bound to a tailor. When the farm came into your hands, your wife died, and you have never looked up since. The land is sold now, but not the house. No! no! you're right enough there; but you've had your troubles, son Thomas, and the lads *are* idle!"

It was the Tailor's mother who spoke. She was a very old woman, and helpless. She was not quite so bright in her intellect as she had been, and got muddled over things that

Juliana Horatia Ewing

had lately happened; but she had a clear memory for what was long past, and was very pertinacious in her opinions. She knew the private history of almost every family in the place, and who of the Trouts were buried under which old stones in the churchyard; and had more tales of ghosts, doubles, warnings, fairies, witches, hobgoblins, and such like, than even her grandchildren had ever come to the end of. Her hands trembled with age, and she regretted this for nothing more than for the danger it brought her into of spilling the salt. She was past housework, but all day she sat knitting hearth-rugs out of the bits and scraps of cloth that were shred in the tailoring. How far she believed in the wonderful tales she told, and the odd little charms she practised, no one exactly knew; but the older she grew, the stranger were the things she remembered, and the more testy she was if any one doubted their truth. "Bairns are a blessing!" said she. "It is the family motto."

"*Are they*?" said the Tailor emphatically.

He had a high respect for his mother, and did not like to contradict her, but he held his own opinion, based upon personal experience; and not being a metaphysician, did not understand that it is safer to found opinions on principles than on experience, since experience may alter, but principles cannot.

"Look at Tommy," he broke out suddenly. "That boy does nothing but whittle sticks from morning till night. I have almost to lug him out of bed o' mornings. If I send him an errand, he loiters; I'd better have gone myself. If I set him to do anything, I have to tell him everything; I could sooner do it myself. And if he does work, it's done so unwillingly, with such a poor grace; better, far better, to do it myself. What housework do the boys ever do but looking after the baby? And this afternoon she was asleep in the cradle, and off they went, and when she awoke, *I* must leave my work to take her. *I* gave her her supper, and put her to bed. And what with what they want and I have to get, and what they take out to play with and lose, and what they bring in to play with and leave about, bairns give some trouble, Mother, and I've not an easy life of it. The pay is poor enough when one can get the work, and the work is hard enough when one has a clear day to do it in; but housekeeping and bairn-minding don't leave a man much time for his trade. No! no! Ma'am, the luck of the Trouts is gone, and 'Bairns are a burden,' is the motto now. Though they are one's own," he muttered to himself, "and not bad ones, and I did hope once would have been a blessing."

"There's Johnnie," murmured the old lady, dreamily. "He has a face like an apple."

"And is about as useful," said the Tailor. "He might have been different, but his brother leads him by the nose."

His brother led him in as the Tailor spoke, not literally by his snub, though, but by the hand. They were a handsome pair, this lazy couple. Johnnie especially had the largest and roundest of foreheads, the reddest of cheeks, the brightest of eyes, the quaintest and most twitchy of chins, and looked altogether like a gutta-percha cherub in a chronic state of longitudinal squeeze. They were locked together by two grubby paws, and had each an armful of moss, which they deposited on the floor as they came in.

"I've swept this floor once to-day," said the father, "and I'm not going to do it again. Put that rubbish outside." "Move it, Johnnie!" said his brother, seating himself on a stool, and taking out his knife and a piece of wood, at which he cut and sliced; while the apple-cheeked Johnnie stumbled and stamped over the moss, and scraped it out on the doorstep, leaving long trails of earth behind him, and then sat down also.

"And those chips the same," added the Tailor; "I will *not* clear up the litter you lads make."

"Pick 'em up, Johnnie," said Thomas Trout, junior, with an exasperated sigh; and the apple tumbled up, rolled after the flying chips, and tumbled down again.

"Is there any supper, Father?" asked Tommy.

"No, there is not, Sir, unless you know how to get it," said the Tailor; and taking his pipe, he went out of the house.

"Is there really nothing to eat, Granny?" asked the boy.

"No, my bairn, only some bread for breakfast to-morrow."

"What makes Father so cross, Granny?"

"He's wearied, and you don't help him, my dear."

"What could I do, Grandmother?"

"Many little things, if you tried," said the old lady. "He spent half-an-hour to-day, while you were on the moor, getting turf for the fire, and you could have got it just as well, and he been at his work."

"He never told me," said Tommy.

"You might help me a bit just now, if you would, my laddie," said the old lady coaxingly; "these bits of cloth want tearing into lengths, and if you get 'em ready, I can go on knitting. There'll be some food when this mat is done and sold."

"I'll try," said Tommy, lounging up with desperate resig-
nation. "Hold my knife, Johnnie. Father's been cross, and
everything has been miserable, ever since the farm was sold.
I wish I were a big man, and could make a fortune.—Will
that do, Granny?"

The old lady put down her knitting and looked. "My dear,
that's too short. Bless me! I gave the lad a piece to measure
by."

"I thought it was the same length. Oh, dear! I am so tired;"
and he propped himself against the old lady's chair.

"My dear! don't lean so; you'll tipple me over!" she shrieked.

"I beg your pardon, Grandmother. Will *that* do?"

"It's that much too long."

"Tear that bit off. Now it's all right."

"But, my dear, that wastes it. Now that bit is of no use. There
goes my knitting, you awkward lad!"

"Johnnie, pick it up!—Oh! Grandmother, I *am* so hungry."
The boy's eyes filled with tears, and the old lady was melted
in an instant.

"What can I do for you, my poor bairns?" said she. "There,
never mind the scraps, Tommy."

"Tell us a tale, Granny. If you told us a new one, I shouldn't
keep thinking of that bread in the cupboard.—Come,
Johnnie, and sit against me. Now then!"

"I doubt if there's one of my old-world cracks I haven't told

Juliana Horatia Ewing

you," said the old lady, "unless it's a queer ghost story was told me years ago of that house in the hollow with the blocked-up windows."

"Oh! not ghosts!" Tommy broke in; "we've had so many. I know it was a rattling, or a scratching, or a knocking, or a figure in white; and if it turns out a tombstone or a white petticoat, I hate it."

"It was nothing of the sort as a tombstone," said the old lady with dignity. "It's a good half-mile from the churchyard. And as to white petticoats, there wasn't a female in the house; he wouldn't have one; and his victuals came in by the pantry window. But never mind! Though it's as true as a sermon."

Johnnie lifted his head from his brother's knee.

"Let Granny tell what she likes, Tommy. It's a new ghost, and I should like to know who he was, and why his victuals came in by the window."

"I don't like a story about victuals," sulked Tommy. "It makes me think of the bread. O Granny dear! do tell us a fairy story. You never will tell us about the Fairies, and I know you know."

"Hush! hush!" said the old lady. "There's Miss Surbiton's Love-letter, and her Dreadful End."

"I know Miss Surbiton, Granny. I think she was a goose. Why don't you tell us about the Fairies?"

"Hush! hush! my dear. There's the Clerk and the Corpse-candles."

"I know the Corpse-candles, Granny. Besides, they make

Johnnie dream, and he wakes me to keep him company. *Why* won't you tell us about the Fairies?"

"My dear, they don't like it," said the old lady.

"O Granny dear, why don't they? Do tell! I shouldn't think of the bread a bit, if you told us about the Fairies. I know nothing about them."

"He lived in this house long enough," said the old lady. "But it's not lucky to name him."

"O Granny, we are so hungry and miserable, what can it matter?"

"Well, that's true enough," she sighed. "Trout's luck is gone; it went with the Brownie, I believe."

"Was that *he*, Granny?"

"Yes, my dear, he lived with the Trouts for several generations."

"What was he like, Granny?"

"Like a little man, they say, my dear."

"What did he do?"

"He came in before the family were up, and swept up the hearth, and lighted the fire, and set out the breakfast, and tidied the room, and did all sorts of house-work. But he never would be seen, and was off before they could catch him. But they could hear him laughing and playing about the house sometimes."

"What a darling! Did they give him any wages, Granny?"

"No! my dear. He did it for love. They set a pancheon of clear water for him over night, and now and then a bowl of bread-and-milk, or cream. He liked that, for he was very dainty. Sometimes he left a bit of money in the water. Sometimes he weeded the garden, or threshed the corn. He saved endless trouble, both to men and maids."

"O Granny! why did he go?"

"The maids caught sight of him one night, my dear, and his coat was so ragged, that they got a new suit, and a linen shirt for him, and laid them by the bread-and-milk bowl. But when Brownie saw the things, he put them on, and dancing round the kitchen, sang,

'What have we here? Hemten hamten!
Here will I never more tread nor stampen,'

and so danced through the door, and never came back again."

"O Grandmother! But why not? Didn't he like the new clothes?"

"The Old Owl knows, my dear; I don't."

"Who's the Old Owl, Granny?"

"I don't exactly know, my dear. It's what my mother used to say when we asked anything that puzzled her. It was said that the Old Owl was Nanny Besom (a witch, my dear!), who took the shape of a bird, but couldn't change her voice, and that's why the owl sits silent all day for fear she should betray herself by speaking, and has no singing voice like other birds. Many people used to go and consult the Old Owl at moon-rise, in my young days."

"Did you ever go, Granny?"

"Once, very nearly, my dear."

"Oh! tell us, Granny dear.—There are no Corpse-candles, Johnnie; it's only moonlight," he added consolingly, as Johnnie crept closer to his knee, and pricked his little red ears.

"It was when your grandfather was courting me, my dears," said the old lady, "and I couldn't quite make up my mind. So I went to my mother, and said, 'He's this on the one side, but then he's that on the other, and so on. Shall I say yes or no?' And my mother said, 'The Old Owl knows;' for she was fairly puzzled. So says I, 'I'll go and ask her to-night, as sure as the moon rises.'

"So at moon-rise I went, and there in the white light by the gate stood your grandfather. 'What are you doing here at this time o' night?' says I. 'Watching your window,' says he. 'What are *you* doing here at this time o' night?' 'The Old Owl knows,' said I, and burst out crying."

"What for?" said Johnnie.

"I can't rightly tell you, my dear," said the old lady, "but it gave me such a turn to see him. And without more ado your grandfather kissed me. 'How dare you?' said I. 'What do you mean?' 'The Old Owl knows,' said he. So we never went."

"How stupid!" said Tommy.

"Tell us more about Brownie, please," said Johnnie, "Did he ever live with anybody else?"

Juliana Horatia Ewing

"There are plenty of Brownies," said the old lady, "or used to be in my mother's young days. Some houses had several." "Oh! I wish ours would come back!" cried both the boys in chorus. "He'd—

"tidy the room," said Johnnie;

"fetch the turf," said Tommy;

"pick up the chips," said Johnnie;

"sort your scraps," said Tommy;

"and do everything. Oh! I wish he hadn't gone away."

"What's that?" said the Tailor, coming in at this moment.

"It's the Brownie, Father," said Tommy. "We are so sorry he went, and do so wish we had one."

"What nonsense have you been telling them, Mother?" asked the Tailor.

"Heighty teighty," said the old lady, bristling. "Nonsense, indeed! As good men as you, son Thomas, would as soon have jumped off the crags, as spoken lightly of *them*, in my mother's young days."

"Well, well," said the Tailor, "I beg their pardon. They never did aught for me, whatever they did for my forbears; but they're as welcome to the old place as ever, if they choose to come. There's plenty to do."

"Would you mind our setting a pan of water, Father?" asked Tommy very gently. "There's no bread-and-milk."

"You may set what you like, my lad," said the Tailor; "and I wish there were bread-and-milk for your sakes, bairns. You should have it, had I got it. But go to bed now."

They lugged out a pancheon, and filled it with more dexterity than usual, and then went off to bed, leaving the knife in one corner, the wood in another, and a few splashes of water in their track.

There was more room than comfort in the ruined old farm-house, and the two boys slept on a bed of cut heather, in what had been the old malt-loft. Johnnie was soon in the land of dreams, growing rosier and rosier as he slept, a tumbled apple among the grey heather. But not so lazy Tommy. The idea of a domesticated Brownie had taken full possession of his mind; and whither Brownie had gone, where he might be found, and what would induce him to return, were mysteries he longed to solve. "There's an owl living in the old shed by the mere," he thought. "It may be the Old Owl herself, and she knows, Granny says. When Father's gone to bed, and the moon rises, I'll go." Meanwhile he lay down.

*　*　*　*　*

The moon rose like gold, and went up into the heavens like silver, flooding the moors with a pale ghostly light, taking the colour out of the heather, and painting black shadows under the stone walls. Tommy opened his eyes, and ran to the window. "The moon has risen," said he, and crept softly down the ladder, through the kitchen, where was the pan of water, but no Brownie, and so out on to the moor. The air was fresh, not to say chilly; but it was a glorious night, though everything but the wind and Tommy seemed asleep. The stones, the walls, the gleaming lanes, were so intensely still; the church tower in the valley seemed awake and watching, but silent; the houses in the village round it had all their eyes shut, that is, their window-blinds down; and it seemed to Tommy as if the very moors had drawn white sheets over them, and lay sleeping also.

"Hoot! hoot!" said a voice from the fir plantation behind him. Somebody else was awake, then. "It's the Old Owl," said Tommy; and there she came, swinging heavily across the moor with a flapping stately flight, and sailed into the shed by the mere. The old lady moved faster than she seemed to do, and though Tommy ran hard she was in the shed some time before him. When he got in, no bird was to be seen, but he heard a crunching sound from above, and looking up, there sat the Old Owl, pecking and tearing and munching at some shapeless black object, and blinking at him—Tommy—with yellow eyes.

"Oh dear!" said Tommy, for he didn't much like it.

The Old Owl dropped the black mass on to the floor; and Tommy did not care somehow to examine it.

"Come up! come up!" said she hoarsely.

She could speak, then! Beyond all doubt it was *the* Old Owl, and none other. Tommy shuddered.

"Come up here! come up here!" said the Old Owl.

The Old Owl sat on a beam that ran across the shed. Tommy had often climbed up for fun; and he climbed up now, and sat face to face with her, and thought her eyes looked as if they were made of flame.

"Kiss my fluffy face," said the Owl.

Her eyes were going round like flaming catherine wheels,

but there are certain requests which one has not the option of refusing. Tommy crept nearer, and put his lips to the round face out of which the eyes shone. Oh! it was so downy and warm, so soft, so indescribably soft. Tommy's lips sank into it, and couldn't get to the bottom. It was unfathomable feathers and fluffiness.

"Now, what do you want?" said the Owl.

"Please," said Tommy, who felt rather re-assured, "can you tell me where to find the Brownies, and how to get one to come and live with us?"

"Oohoo!" said the Owl, "that's it, is it? I know of three Brownies."

"Hurrah!" said Tommy. "Where do they live?"

"In your house," said the Owl.

Tommy was aghast.

"In our house!" he exclaimed. "Whereabouts? Let me rummage them out. Why do they do nothing?"

"One of them is too young," said the Owl.

"But why don't the others work?" asked Tommy.

"They are idle, they are idle," said the Old Owl, and she gave herself such a shake as she said it, that the fluff went flying through the shed, and Tommy nearly tumbled off the beam in his fright.

"Then we don't want them," said he. "What is the use of having Brownies if they do nothing to help us?"

Juliana Horatia Ewing

"Perhaps they don't know how, as no one has told them," said the Owl.

"I wish you would tell me where to find them," said Tommy; "I could tell them."

"Could you?" said the Owl. "Oohoo! oohoo!" and Tommy couldn't tell whether she were hooting or laughing.

"Of course I could," he said. "They might be up and sweep the house, and light the fire, and spread the table, and that sort of thing, before Father came down. Besides, they could *see* what was wanted. The Brownies did all that in Granny's mother's young days. And then they could tidy the room, and fetch the turf, and pick up my chips, and sort Granny's scraps. Oh! there's lots to do."

"So there is," said the Owl. "Oohoo! Well, I can tell you where to find one of the Brownies; and if you find him, he will tell you where his brother is. But all this depends upon whether you feel equal to undertaking it, and whether you will follow my directions."

"I am quite ready to go," said Tommy, "and I will do as you shall tell me. I feel sure I could persuade them. If they only knew how every one would love them if they made themselves useful!"

"Oohoo! oohoo!" said the Owl. "Now pay attention. You must go to the north side of the mere when the moon is shining—('I know Brownies like water,' muttered Tommy)—and turn yourself round three times, saying this charm:

'Twist me, and turn me, and show me the Elf—
I looked in the water, and saw—'

When you have got so far, look into the water, and at the same moment you will see the Brownie, and think of a word that will fill up the couplet, and rhyme with the first line. If either you do not see the Brownie, or fail to think of the word, it will be of no use."

"Is the Brownie a merman," said Tommy, wriggling himself along the beam, "that he lives under water?"

"That depends on whether he has a fish's tail," said the Owl, "and this you can discover for yourself."

"Well, the moon is shining, so I shall go," said Tommy. "Good-bye, and thank you, Ma'am;" and he jumped down and went, saying to himself as he ran, "I believe he is a merman all the same, or else how could he live in the mere? I know more about Brownies than Granny does, and I shall tell her so;" for Tommy was somewhat opinionated, like other young people.

The moon shone very brightly on the centre of the mere. Tommy knew the place well, for there was a fine echo there. Round the edge grew rushes and water plants, which cast a border of shadow. Tommy went to the north side, and turning himself three times, as the Old Owl had told him, he repeated the charm—

"Twist me, and turn me, and show me the Elf—
I looked in the water, and saw—"

Now for it! He looked in, and saw—the reflection of his own face.

"Why, there's no one but myself!" said Tommy. "And what can the word be? I must have done it wrong."

Juliana Horatia Ewing

"Wrong!" said the Echo.

Tommy was almost surprised to find the echo awake at this time of night.

"Hold your tongue!" said he. "Matters are provoking enough of themselves. Belf! Celf! Delf! Felf! Gelf! Helf! Jelf! What rubbish! There can't be a word to fit it. And then to look for a Brownie, and see nothing but myself!"

"Myself," said the Echo.

"Will you be quiet?" said Tommy. "If you would tell one the word there would be some sense in your interference; but to roar 'Myself!' at one, which neither rhymes nor runs—it does rhyme though, as it happens," he added; "and how very odd! it runs too—

'Twist me, and turn me, and show me the Elf—
I looked in the water, and saw myself,'

which I certainly did. What can it mean? The Old Owl knows, as Granny would say; so I shall go back and ask her."

"Ask her!" said the Echo.

"Didn't I say I should?" said Tommy. "How exasperating you are! It is very strange. *Myself* certainly does rhyme, and I wonder I did not think of it long ago."

"Go," said the Echo.

"Will you mind your own business, and go to sleep?" said Tommy. "I am going; I said I should."

And back he went. There sat the Old Owl as before.

"Oohoo!" said she, as Tommy climbed up. "What did you see in the mere?"

"I saw nothing but myself," said Tommy indignantly.

"And what did you expect to see?" asked the Owl.

"I expected to see a Brownie," said Tommy; "you told me so."

"And what are Brownies like, pray?" inquired the Owl.

"The one Granny knew was a useful little fellow, something like a little man," said Tommy.

"Ah!" said the Owl, "but you know at present this one is an idle little fellow, something like a little man. Oohoo! oohoo! Are you quite sure you didn't see him?"

"Quite," answered Tommy sharply. "I saw no one but myself."

"Hoot! toot! How touchy we are! And who are you, pray?"

"I'm not a Brownie," said Tommy.

"Don't be too sure," said the Owl. "Did you find out the word?"

"No," said Tommy. "I could find no word with any meaning that would rhyme but 'myself.'"

"Well, that runs and rhymes," said the Owl. "What do you want? Where's your brother now?"

"In bed in the malt-loft," said Tommy.

"Then now all your questions are answered," said the Owl, "and you know what wants doing, so go and do it. Good-night, or rather good-morning, for it is long past midnight;" and the old lady began to shake her feathers for a start.

"Don't go yet, please," said Tommy humbly. "I don't understand it. You know I'm not a Brownie, am I?"

"Yes, you are," said the Owl, "and a very idle one too. All children are Brownies."

"But I couldn't do work like a Brownie," said Tommy.

"Why not?" inquired the Owl. "Couldn't you sweep the floor, light the fire, spread the table, tidy the room, fetch the turf, pick up your own chips, and sort your grandmother's scraps? You know 'there's lots to do.'"

"But I don't think I should like it," said Tommy. "I'd much rather have a Brownie to do it for me."

"And what would you do meanwhile?" asked the Owl. "Be idle, I suppose; and what do you suppose is the use of a man's having children if they do nothing to help him? Ah! if they only knew how every one would love them if they made themselves useful!"

"But is it really and truly so?" asked Tommy, in a dismal voice. "Are there no Brownies but children?"

"No, there are not," said the Owl. "And pray do you think that the Brownies, whoever they may be, come into the house to save trouble for the idle healthy little boys who live in it? Listen to me, Tommy," said the old lady, her eyes shooting rays of fire in the dark corner where she sat. "Listen to me, you are a clever boy, and can understand when one speaks; so I will tell you the whole history of the Brownies, as it has been handed down in our family from my grandmother's great-grandmother, who lived in the Druid's Oak, and was intimate with the fairies. And when I have done you shall tell me what you think they are, if they are not children. It's the opinion I have come to at any rate, and I don't think that wisdom died with our great-grandmothers."

"I should like to hear if you please," said Tommy.

The Old Owl shook out a tuft or two of fluff, and set her eyes a-going and began:

"The Brownies, or, as they are sometimes called, the Small Folk, the Little People, or the Good People, are a race of tiny beings who domesticate themselves in a house of which some grown-up human being pays the rent and taxes. They are like small editions of men and women, they are too small and fragile for heavy work; they have not the strength of a man, but are a thousand times more fresh and nimble. They can run and jump, and roll and tumble, with marvellous agility and endurance, and of many of the aches and pains which men and women groan under, they do not even know the names. They have no trade or profession, and as they live entirely upon other people, they know nothing of domestic cares; in fact, they know very little upon any subject, though they are often intelligent and highly inquisitive. They love dainties, play, and mischief. They are apt to be greatly beloved, and are themselves capriciously affectionate. They are little people, and can only do little things. When they are idle and mischievous, they are called Boggarts, and are a curse to the house they live in. When they are useful and considerate, they are Brownies, and are a much-coveted blessing. Sometimes the Blessed Brownies will take up their abode with some worthy couple, cheer them with their romps and merry laughter, tidy the house, find things that have been lost, and take little troubles out of hands full of great anxieties. Then in time these Little People are Brownies no longer. They grow up into men and women. They do not care so much for dainties, play, or mischief. They cease to jump and tumble, and roll about the house. They know more, and laugh less. Then, when their heads begin to ache with anxiety, and they have to labour for their own living, and the great cares of life come on, other Brownies come and live with them, and take up their little cares, and supply their little comforts, and make the house merry once more."

"How nice!" said Tommy.

"Very nice," said the Old Owl. "But what"—and she shook herself more fiercely than ever, and glared so that Tommy expected nothing less than that her eyes would set fire to her feathers and she would be burnt alive. "But what must I say of the Boggarts? Those idle urchins who eat the bread-and-milk, and don't do the work, who lie in bed without an ache or pain to excuse them, who untidy instead of tidying, cause work instead of doing it, and leave little cares to heap on big cares, till the old people who support them are worn out altogether."

"Don't!" said Tommy. "I can't bear it."

"I hope when Boggarts grow into men," said the Old Owl, "that their children will be Boggarts too, and then they'll know what it is!"

"Don't!" roared Tommy. "I won't be a Boggart. I'll be a Brownie."

"That's right," nodded the Old Owl. "I said you were a boy who could understand when one spoke. And remember that the Brownies never are seen at their work. They get up before the household, and get away before any one can see them. I can't tell you why. I don't think my grandmother's great-grandmother knew. Perhaps because all good deeds are better done in secret."

"Please," said Tommy, "I should like to go home now, and tell Johnnie. It's getting cold, and I am so tired!"

"Very true," said the Old Owl, "and then you will have to be up early to-morrow. I think I had better take you home."

"I know the way, thank you," said Tommy.

"I didn't say *show* you the way, I said *take* you—carry you," said the Owl. "Lean against me."

"I'd rather not, thank you," said Tommy.

"Lean against me," screamed the Owl. "Oohoo! how obstinate boys are to be sure!"

Tommy crept up very unwillingly.

"Lean your full weight, and shut your eyes," said the Owl.

Tommy laid his head against the Old Owl's feathers, had a vague idea that she smelt of heather, and thought it must be from living on the moor, shut his eyes, and leant his full weight, expecting that he and the Owl would certainly fall off the beam together. Down—feathers—fluff—he sank and sank, could feel nothing solid, jumped up with a start to save himself, opened his eyes, and found that he was sitting among the heather in the malt-loft, with Johnnie sleeping by his side.

"How quickly we came!" said he; "that is certainly a very

clever Old Owl. I couldn't have counted ten whilst my eyes were shut. How very odd!"

But what was odder still was, that it was no longer moonlight, but early dawn.

"Get up, Johnnie," said his brother, "I've got a story to tell you."

And while Johnnie sat up, and rubbed his eyes open, he related his adventures on the moor.

"Is all that true?" said Johnnie. "I mean, did it really happen?"

"Of course it did," said his brother; "don't you believe it?"

"Oh yes," said Johnnie. "But I thought it was perhaps only a true story, like Granny's true stories. I believe all those, you know. But if you were there, you know, it is different—"

"I was there," said Tommy, "and it's all just as I tell you: and I tell you what, if we mean to do anything we must get up: though, oh dear! I should like to stay in bed. I say," he added, after a pause, "suppose we do. It can't matter being Boggarts for one night more. I mean to be a Brownie before I grow up, though. I couldn't stand boggarty children."

"I won't be a Boggart at all," said Johnnie, "it's horrid. But I don't see how we can be Brownies, for I'm afraid we can't do the things. I wish I were bigger!"

"I can do it well enough," said Tommy, following his brother's example and getting up. "Don't you suppose I can light a fire? Think of all the bonfires we have made! And I don't think I should mind having a regular good tidy-up either. It's that stupid putting-away-things-when-you've-done-with-them that I hate so!"

The Brownies crept softly down the ladder and into the kitchen. There was the blank hearth, the dirty floor, and all the odds and ends lying about, looking cheerless enough in the dim light. Tommy felt quite important as he looked round. There is no such cure for untidiness as clearing up after other people; one sees so clearly where the fault lies.

"Look at that door-step, Johnnie," said the Brownie-elect, "what a mess you made of it! If you had lifted the moss carefully, instead of stamping and struggling with it, it would have saved us ten minutes' work this morning."

This wisdom could not be gainsaid, and Johnnie only looked meek and rueful.

"I am going to light the fire," pursued his brother;—"the next turfs, you know, *we* must get—you can tidy a bit. Look at that knife I gave you to hold last night, and that wood—that's my fault though, and so are those scraps by Granny's chair. What are you grubbing at that rat-hole for?"

Johnnie raised his head somewhat flushed and tumbled.

"What do you think I have found?" said he triumphantly. "Father's measure that has been lost for a week!"

"Hurrah!" said Tommy, "put it by his things. That's just a sort of thing for a Brownie to have done. What will he say? And I say, Johnnie, when you've tidied, just go and grub up a potato or two in the garden, and I'll put them to roast for breakfast. I'm lighting such a bonfire!"

The fire was very successful. Johnnie went after the potatoes, and Tommy cleaned the door-step, swept the room, dusted the chairs and the old chest, and set out the table. There was no doubt he could be handy when he chose.

"I'll tell you what I've thought of, if we have time," said Johnnie, as he washed the potatoes in the water that had been set for Brownie. "We might run down to the South Pasture for some mushrooms. Father said the reason we found so few was that people go by sunrise for them to take to market. The sun's only just rising, we should be sure to find some, and they would do for breakfast."

"There's plenty of time," said Tommy; so they went. The dew lay heavy and thick upon the grass by the road-side, and over the miles of network that the spiders had woven from blossom to blossom of the heather. The dew is the Sun's breakfast; but he was barely up yet, and had not eaten it, and the world felt anything but warm. Nevertheless, it was so sweet and fresh as it is at no later hour of the day, and every sound was like the returning voice of a long-absent friend. Down to the pastures, where was more network and more dew, but when one has nothing to speak of in the way of boots, the state of the ground is of the less consequence.

The Tailor had been right, there was no lack of mushrooms at this time of the morning. All over the pasture they stood, of all sizes, some like buttons, some like tables; and in the distance one or two ragged women, stooping over them with baskets, looked like huge fungi also.

"This is where the fairies feast," said Tommy. "They had a large party last night. When they go, they take away the dishes and cups, for they are made of gold; but they leave their tables, and we eat them."

"I wonder whether giants would like to eat our tables,"

said Johnnie.

This was beyond Tommy's capabilities of surmise; so they filled a handkerchief, and hurried back again, for fear the Tailor should have come down-stairs.

They were depositing the last mushroom in a dish on the table, when his footsteps were heard descending.

"There he is!" exclaimed Tommy. "Remember, we mustn't be caught. Run back to bed."

Johnnie caught up the handkerchief, and smothering their laughter, the two scrambled back up the ladder, and dashed straight into the heather.

Meanwhile the poor Tailor came wearily down-stairs. Day after day, since his wife's death, he had come down every morning to the same desolate sight—yesterday's refuse and an empty hearth. This morning task of tidying was always a sad and ungrateful one to the widowed father. His awkward struggles with the house-work in which *she* had been so notable, chafed him. The dirty kitchen was dreary, the labour lonely, and it was an hour's time lost to his trade. But life does not stand still while one is wishing, and so the Tailor did that for which there was neither remedy nor substitute; and came down this morning as other mornings to the pail and broom. When he came in he looked round, and started, and rubbed his eyes; looked round again, and rubbed them harder: then went up to the fire and held out his hand, (warm certainly)—then up to the table and smelt the mushrooms, (esculent fungi beyond a doubt)—handled the loaf, stared at the open door and window, the swept floor, and the sunshine pouring in, and finally sat down in stunned admiration. Then he jumped up and ran to the foot of the stairs, shouting,

"Mother! mother! Trout's luck has come again." "And yet, no!" he thought, "the old lady's asleep, it's a shame to wake her, I'll tell those idle rascally lads, they'll be more pleased than they deserve. It was Tommy after all that set the water and caught him." "Boys! boys!" he shouted at the foot of the ladder, "the Brownie has come!—and if he hasn't found my measure!" he added on returning to the kitchen; "this is as good as a day's work to me."

There was great excitement in the small household that day. The boys kept their own counsel. The old Grandmother was triumphant, and tried not to seem surprised. The Tailor made no such vain effort, and remained till bed-time in a state of fresh and unconcealed amazement.

"I've often heard of the Good People," he broke out towards the end of the evening. "And I've heard folk say they've known those that have seen them capering round the grey rocks on the moor at midnight: but this is wonderful! To come and do the work for a pan of cold water! Who could have believed it?"

"You might have believed it if you'd believed me, son Thomas," said the old lady tossily. "I told you so. But young people always know better than their elders!"

"I didn't see him," said the Tailor, beginning his story afresh; "but I thought as I came in I heard a sort of laughing and rustling."

"My mother said they often heard him playing and laughing about the house," said the old lady. "I told you so."

"Well, he sha'n't want for a bowl of bread-and-milk to-morrow, anyhow," said the Tailor, "if I have to stick to Farmer Swede's waistcoat till midnight."

But the waistcoat was finished by bed-time, and the Tailor set the bread-and-milk himself, and went to rest.

"I say," said Tommy, when both the boys were in bed, "the Old Owl was right, and we must stick to it. But I'll tell you what I don't like, and that is Father thinking we're idle still. I wish he knew we were the Brownies."

"So do I," said Johnnie; and he sighed.

"I tell you what," said Tommy, with the decisiveness of elder brotherhood, "we'll keep quiet for a bit for fear we should leave off; but when we've gone on a good while, I shall tell him. It was only the Old Owl's grandmother's great-grandmother who said it was to be kept secret, and the Old Owl herself said grandmothers were not always in the right."

"No more they are," said Johnnie; "look at Granny about this."

"I know," said Tommy. "She's in a regular muddle."

"So she is," said Johnnie. "But that's rather fun, I think."

And they went to sleep.

Day after day went by, and still the Brownies "stuck to it," and did their work. It is no such very hard matter after all to get up early when one is young and light-hearted, and sleeps upon heather in a loft without window-blinds, and with so many broken window-panes that the air comes freely in. In old times the boys used to play at tents among the heather, while the Tailor did the house-work; now they came down and did it for him.

Size is not everything, even in this material existence. One has heard of dwarfs who were quite as clever (not to say as powerful) as giants, and I do not fancy that Fairy God-mothers are ever very large. It is wonderful what a comfort Brownies may be in the house that is fortunate enough to hold them! The Tailor's Brownies were the joy of his life; and day after day they seemed to grow more and more ingenious in finding little things to do for his good.

Now-a-days Granny never picked a scrap for herself. One day's shearings were all neatly arranged the next morning, and laid by her knitting-pins; and the Tailor's tape and shears were no more absent without leave.

One day a message came to him to offer him two or three days' tailoring in a farm-house some miles up the valley. This was pleasant and advantageous sort of work; good food, sure pay, and a cheerful change; but he did not know how he could leave his family, unless, indeed, the Brownie might be relied upon to "keep the house together," as they say. The boys were sure that he would, and they promised to set his water, and to give as little trouble as possible; so, finally, the Tailor took up his shears and went up the valley, where the green banks sloped up into purple moor, or broke into sandy rocks, crowned with nodding oak fern. On to the prosperous old farm, where he spent a very pleasant time, sitting level with the window geraniums on a table set apart for him, stitching and gossiping, gossiping and stitching, and feeling secure of honest payment when his work was done. The mistress of the house was a kind good creature, and loved a chat; and though the Tailor kept his own secret as to the Brownies, he felt rather curious to know if the Good People had any hand in the comfort of this flourishing household, and watched his opportunity to make a few careless inquiries on the subject.

"Brownies?" laughed the dame. "Ay, Master, I have heard of

them. When I was a girl, in service at the old hall, on Cowberry Edge, I heard a good deal of one they said had lived there in former times. He did house-work as well as a woman, and a good deal quicker, they said. One night one of the young ladies (that were then, they're all dead now) hid herself in a cupboard, to see what he was like."

"And what was he like?" inquired the Tailor, as composedly as he was able.

"A little fellow, they said," answered the Farmer's wife, knitting calmly on. "Like a dwarf, you know, with a largish head for his body. Not taller than—why, my Bill, or your eldest boy, perhaps. And he was dressed in rags, with an old cloak on, and stamping with passion at a cobweb he couldn't get at with his broom. They've very uncertain tempers, they say. Tears one minute, and laughing the next."

"You never had one here, I suppose?" said the Tailor.

"Not we," she answered; "and I think I'd rather not. They're not canny after all; and my master and me have always been used to work, and we've sons and daughters to help us, and that's better than meddling with the Fairies, to my mind. No! no!" she added, laughing, "if we had had one you'd have heard of it, whoever didn't, for I should have had some decent clothes made for him. I couldn't stand rags and old cloaks, messing and moth-catching, in my house."

"They say it's not lucky to give them clothes, though," said the Tailor; "they don't like it."

"Tell me!" said the dame, "as if any one that liked a tidy room wouldn't like tidy clothes, if they could get them. No! no! when we have one, you shall take his measure, I promise you."

Juliana Horatia Ewing

And this was all the Tailor got out of her on the subject. When his work was finished, the Farmer paid him at once; and the good dame added half a cheese, and a bottle-green coat.

"That has been laid by for being too small for the master now he's so stout," she said; "but except for a stain or two it's good enough, and will cut up like new for one of the lads."

The Tailor thanked them, and said farewell, and went home. Down the valley, where the river, wandering between the green banks and the sandy rocks, was caught by giant mosses, and bands of fairy fern, and there choked and struggled, and at last barely escaped with an existence, and ran away in a diminished stream. On up the purple hills to the old ruined house. As he came in at the gate he was struck by some idea of change, and looking again, he saw that the garden had been weeded, and was comparatively tidy. The truth is, that Tommy and Johnnie had taken advantage of the Tailor's absence to do some Brownie's work in the daytime.

"It's that Blessed Brownie!" said the Tailor. "Has he been as usual?" he asked, when he was in the house.

"To be sure," said the old lady; "all has been well, son Thomas."

"I'll tell you what it is," said the Tailor, after a pause. "I'm a needy man, but I hope I'm not ungrateful. I can never repay the Brownie for what he has done for me and mine; but the mistress up yonder has given me a bottle-green coat that will cut up as good as new; and as sure as there's a Brownie in this house, I'll make him a suit of it."

"You'll *what*?" shrieked the old lady. "Son Thomas, son Thomas, you're mad! Do what you please for the Brownies, but never make them clothes."

"There's nothing they want more," said the Tailor, "by all accounts. They're all in rags, as well they may be, doing so much work."

"If you make clothes for this Brownie, he'll go for good," said the Grandmother, in a voice of awful warning.

"Well, I don't know," said her son. "The mistress up at the farm is clever enough, I can tell you; and as she said to me, fancy any one that likes a tidy room not liking a tidy coat!" For the Tailor, like most men, was apt to think well of the wisdom of womankind in other houses.

"Well, well," said the old lady, "go your own way. I'm an old woman, and my time is not long. It doesn't matter much to me. But it was new clothes that drove the Brownie out before, and Trout's luck went with him."

"I know, Mother," said the Tailor, "and I've been thinking of it all the way home; and I can tell you why it was. Depend upon it, *the clothes didn't fit*. But I'll tell you what I mean to do. I shall measure them by Tommy—they say the Brownies are about his size—and if ever I turned out a well-made coat and waistcoat, they shall be his."

"Please yourself," said the old lady, and she would say no more.

"I think you're quite right, Father," said Tommy, "and if I can, I'll help you to make them."

Next day the father and son set to work, and Tommy contrived to make himself so useful, that the Tailor hardly knew how he got through so much work.

Juliana Horatia Ewing

"It's not like the same thing," he broke out at last, "to have some one a bit helpful about you; both for the tailoring and for company's sake. I've not done such a pleasant morning's work since your poor mother died. I'll tell you what it is, Tommy," he added, "if you were always like this, I shouldn't much care whether Brownie stayed or went. I'd give up his help to have yours."

"I'll be back directly," said Tommy, who burst out of the room in search of his brother.

"I've come away," he said, squatting down, "because I can't bear it. I very nearly let it all out, and I shall soon. I wish the things weren't going to come to me," he added, kicking a stone in front of him. "I wish he'd measured you, Johnnie."

"I'm very glad he didn't," said Johnnie. "I wish he'd kept them himself."

"Bottle-green, with brass buttons," murmured Tommy, and therewith fell into a reverie.

The next night the suit was finished, and laid by the bread-and-milk.

"We shall see," said the old lady, in a withering tone. There is not much real prophetic wisdom in this truism, but it sounds very awful, and the Tailor went to bed somewhat depressed.

Next morning the Brownies came down as usual.

"Don't they look splendid?" said Tommy, feeling the cloth. "When we've tidied the place I shall put them on."

But long before the place was tidy, he could wait no longer, and dressed up.

"Look at me!" he shouted; "bottle-green and brass buttons! Oh, Johnnie, I wish you had some."

"It's a good thing there are two Brownies," said Johnnie, laughing, "and one of them in rags still. I shall do the work this morning." And he went flourishing round with a broom, while Tommy jumped madly about in his new suit. "Hurrah!" he shouted, "I feel just like the Brownie. What was it Granny said he sang when he got his clothes? Oh, I know—

'What have we here? Hemten hamten!
Here will I never more tread nor stampen.'"

And on he danced, regardless of the clouds of dust raised by Johnnie, as he drove the broom indiscriminately over the floor, to the tune of his own laughter.

It was laughter which roused the Tailor that morning, laughter coming through the floor from the kitchen below. He scrambled on his things and stole down-stairs.

"It's the Brownie," he thought; "I must look, if it's for the last time."

At the door he paused and listened. The laughter was mixed with singing, and he heard the words—

"What have we here? Hemten hamten!
Here will I never more tread nor stampen."

He pushed in, and this was the sight that met his eyes.

The kitchen in its primeval condition of chaos, the untidy

particulars of which were the less apparent, as everything was more or less obscured by the clouds of dust, where Johnnie reigned triumphant, like a witch with her broomstick; and, to crown all, Tommy capering and singing in the Brownie's bottle-green suit, brass buttons and all.

"What's this?" shouted the astonished Tailor, when he could find breath to speak.

"It's the Brownies," sang the boys; and on they danced, for they had worked themselves up into a state of excitement from which it was not easy to settle down.

"Where *is* Brownie?" shouted the father.

"He's here," said Tommy; "we are the Brownies."

"Can't you stop that fooling?" cried the Tailor, angrily. "This is past a joke. Where is the real Brownie, I say?"

"We are the only Brownies, really, Father," said Tommy, coming to a full stop, and feeling strongly tempted to run down from laughing to crying. "Ask the Old Owl. It's true, really."

The Tailor saw the boy was in earnest, and passed his hand over his forehead.

"I suppose I'm getting old," he said; "I can't see daylight through this. If you are the Brownie, who has been tidying the kitchen lately?"

"We have," said they.

"But who found my measure?"

"I did," said Johnnie.

"And who sorts your grandmother's scraps?"

"We do," said they.

"And who sets breakfast, and puts my things in order?"

"We do," said they.

"But when do you do it?" asked the Tailor.

"Before you come down," said they.

"But I always have to call you," said the Tailor.

"We get back to bed again," said the boys.

"But how was it you never did it before?" asked the Tailor doubtfully.

"We were idle, we were idle," said Tommy.

The Tailor's voice rose to a pitch of desperation—

"But if you did the work," he shouted, "*where is the Brownie?*"

"Here!" cried the boys, "and we are very sorry that we were Boggarts so long."

With which the father and sons fell into each other's arms and fairly wept.

*   *   *   *   *

Juliana Horatia Ewing

It will be believed that to explain all this to the Grandmother was not the work of a moment. She understood it all at last, however, and the Tailor could not restrain a little good-humoured triumph on the subject. Before he went to work he settled her down in the window with her knitting, and kissed her.

"What do you think of it all, Mother?" he inquired.

"Bairns are a blessing," said the old lady tartly, "*I told you so.*"

*   *   *   *   *

"That's not the end, is it?" asked one of the boys in a tone of dismay, for the Doctor had paused here.

"Yes, it is," said he.

"But couldn't you make a little more end?" asked Deordie, "to tell us what became of them all?"

"I don't see what there is to tell," said the Doctor.

"Why, there's whether they ever saw the Old Owl again, and whether Tommy and Johnnie went on being Brownies," said the children.

The Doctor laughed.

"Well, be quiet for five minutes," he said.

"We'll be as quiet as mice," said the children.

And as quiet as mice they were. Very like mice, indeed. Very like mice behind a wainscot at night, when you have just thrown something to frighten them away. Death-like stillness for a few seconds, and then all the rustling and scuffling you please. So the children sat holding their breath for a moment or two, and then shuffling feet and smothered bursts of laughter testified to their impatience, and to the difficulty of understanding the process of story-making as displayed by the Doctor, who sat pulling his beard, and staring at his boots, as he made up "a little more end."

"Well," he said, sitting up suddenly, "the Brownies went on with their work in spite of the bottle-green suit, and Trout's luck returned to the old house once more. Before long Tommy began to work for the farmers, and Baby grew up into a Brownie, and made (as girls are apt to make) the best house-sprite of all. For, in the Brownie's habits of self-denial, thoughtfulness, consideration, and the art of little kindnesses, boys are, I am afraid, as a general rule, somewhat behind-hand with their sisters. Whether this altogether proceeds from constitutional deficiency on these points in the masculine character, or is one result among many of the code of bye-laws which obtains in men's moral education from the cradle, is a question on which everybody has their own opinion. For the present the young gentlemen may appropriate whichever theory they prefer, and we will go back to the story. The Tailor lived to see his boy-Brownies become men, with all the cares of a prosperous farm on their hands, and his girl-Brownie carry her fairy talents into another home. For these Brownies—young ladies!—are much desired as wives, whereas a man might as well marry an old witch as a young Boggartess."

"And about the Owl?" clamoured the children, rather resent-ful of the Doctor's pausing to take breath.

"Of course," he continued, "the Tailor heard the whole story, and being both anxious to thank the Old Owl for her friendly offices, and also rather curious to see and hear her, he went with the boys one night at moon-rise to the shed by the mere. It was earlier in the evening than when Tommy went, for before daylight had vanished, and at the first appearance of the moon, the impatient Tailor was at the place. There they found the Owl looking very solemn and stately on the beam. She was sitting among the shadows with her shoulders up, and she fixed her eyes so steadily on the Tailor, that he felt quite overpowered. He made her a civil bow, however, and said,

"I'm much obliged to you, Ma'am, for your good advice to my Tommy."

The Owl blinked sharply, as if she grudged shutting her eyes for an instant, and then stared on, but not a word spoke she.

"I don't mean to intrude, Ma'am," said the Tailor, "but I was wishful to pay my respects and gratitude."

Still the Owl gazed in determined silence.

"Don't you remember me?" said Tommy pitifully. "I did everything you told me. Won't you even say good-bye?" and he went up towards her.

The Owl's eyes contracted, she shuddered a few tufts of fluff into the shed, shook her wings, and shouting "Oohoo!" at the top of her voice, flew out upon the moor. The Tailor and his sons rushed out to watch her. They could see her clearly against the green twilight sky, flapping rapidly away with her round face to the pale moon. "Good-bye!" they shouted as she disappeared; first the departing owl, then a shadowy body with flapping sails, then two wings beating the same measured time, then two moving lines still to the old tune, then a stroke, a fancy, and then—the green sky and the pale moon, but the Old Owl was gone.

"Did she never come back?" asked Tiny in subdued tones, for the Doctor had paused again.

"No," said he; "at least not to the shed by the mere. Tommy saw many owls after this in the course of his life; but as none of them would speak, and as most of them were addicted to the unconventional customs of staring and winking, he could not distinguish his friend, if she were among them. And now I think that is all."

"Is that the very very end?" asked Tiny.

"The very very end," said the Doctor.

"I suppose there might be more and more ends," speculated Deordie—"about whether the Brownies had any children when they grew into farmers, and whether the children were Brownies, and whether *they* had other Brownies, and so on and on." And Deordie rocked himself among the geraniums, in the luxurious imagining of an endless fairy tale.

"You insatiable rascal!" said the Doctor. "Not another word. Jump up, for I am going to see you home. I have to be off early to-morrow."

"Where?" said Deordie.

"Never mind. I shall be away all day, and I want to be at home in good time in the evening, for I mean to attack that crop of groundsel between the sweet-pea hedges. You know, no Brownies come to my homestead!"

And the Doctor's mouth twitched a little till he fixed it into a stiff smile.

The children tried hard to extract some more ends out of him on the way to the Rectory; but he declined to pursue the history of the Trout family through indefinite generations. It was decided on all hands, however, that Tommy Trout was evidently one and the same with the Tommy Trout who pulled the cat out of the well, because "it was just a sort of thing for a Brownie to do, you know!" and that Johnnie Green (who, of course, was not Johnnie Trout) was some unworthy village acquaintance, and "a thorough Boggart."

"Doctor!" said Tiny, as they stood by the garden-gate, "how long do you think gentlemen's pocket-handkerchiefs take to wear out?"

"That, my dear Madam," said the Doctor, "must depend, like other terrestrial matters, upon circumstances; whether the gentleman bought fine cambric, or coarse cotton with pink portraits of the reigning Sovereign, to commence with; whether he catches many colds, has his pockets picked, takes snuff, or allows his washerwoman to use washing powders. But why do you want to know?"

"I sha'n't tell you that," said Tiny, who was spoilt by the Doctor, and consequently tyrannized in proportion; "but I will tell you what I mean to do. I mean to tell Mother that when Father wants any more pocket-handkerchiefs hemmed, she had better put them by the bath in the nursery, and perhaps some Brownie will come and do them."

"Kiss my fluffy face!" said the Doctor in sepulchral tones.

"The owl is too high up," said Tiny, tossing her head.

The Doctor lifted her four feet or so, obtained his kiss, and set her down again.

"You're not fluffy at all," said she in a tone of the utmost contempt; "you're tickly and bristly. Puss is more fluffy, and Father is scrubby and scratchy, because he shaves."

"And which of the three styles do you prefer?" said the Doctor.

"Not tickly and bristly," said Tiny with firmness; and she strutted up the walk for a space or two, and then turned round to laugh over her shoulder.

"Good-night!" shouted her victim, shaking his fist after her.

The other children took a noisy farewell, and they all raced into the house to give joint versions of the fairy tale, first to the parents in the drawing-room, and then to Nurse in the nursery.

The Doctor went home also, with his poodle at his heels, but not by the way he came. He went out of his way, which was odd; but then the Doctor was "a little odd," and moreover this was always the end of his evening walk. Through the church-yard, where spreading cedars and stiff yews rose from the velvet grass, and where among tombstones and crosses of various devices lay one of older and uglier date, by which he stayed. It was framed by a border of the most brilliant flowers, and it would seem as if the Doctor must have been the gardener, for he picked off some dead ones, and put them absently in his pocket. Then he looked round as if to see that he was alone. Not a soul was to be seen, and the moonlight and shadow lay quietly side by side, as the dead do in their graves. The Doctor stooped down and took off his hat.

"Good-night, Marcia," he said in a low quiet voice. "Good-night, my darling!" The dog licked his hand, but there was no voice to answer, nor any that regarded.

Poor foolish Doctor! Most foolish to speak to the departed with his face earthwards. But we are weak mortals, the best of us; and this man (one of the very best) raised his head at last, and went home like a lonely owl with his face to the moon and the sky.

A BORROWED BROWNIE.

"I can't imagine," said the Rector, walking into the drawing-room the following afternoon; "I can't imagine where Tiny is. I want her to drive to the other end of the parish with me."

"There she comes," said his wife, looking out of the window, "by the garden-gate, with a great basket; what has she been after?"

The Rector went out to discover, and met his daughter looking decidedly earthy, and seemingly much exhausted by the weight of a basketful of groundsel plants.

"Where have you been?" said he.

"In the Doctor's garden," said Tiny triumphantly; "and look what I have done! I've weeded his sweet-peas, and brought away the groundsel; so when he gets home to-night he'll think a Brownie has been in the garden, for Mrs. Pickles has promised not to tell him."

"But look here!" said the Rector, affecting a great appearance of severity, "you're my Brownie, not his. Supposing Tommy Trout had gone and weeded Farmer Swede's garden, and brought back his weeds to go to seed on the Tailor's flower-beds, how do you think he would have liked it?"

Tiny looked rather crestfallen. When one has fairly carried through a splendid benevolence of this kind, it is trying to find oneself in the wrong. She crept up to the Rector, however, and put her golden head upon his arm.

"But, Father dear," she pleaded, "I didn't mean not to be your Brownie; only, you know, you had got five left at home, and it was only for a short time, and the Doctor hasn't any Brownie at all. Don't you pity him?"

And the Rector, who was old enough to remember that grave-stone story we wot of, hugged his Brownie in his arms, and answered,

"My Darling, I do pity him!"

THE LAND OF LOST TOYS

AN EARTHQUAKE IN THE NURSERY

It was certainly an aggravated offence. It is generally understood in families that "boys will be boys," but there is a limit to the forbearance implied in the extenuating axiom. Master Sam was condemned to the back nursery for the rest of the day.

He always had had the knack of breaking his own toys,—he not unfrequently broke other people's; but accidents will happen, and his twin-sister and factotum, Dot, was long-suffering.

Dot was fat, resolute, hasty, and devotedly unselfish. When Sam scalped her new doll, and fastened the glossy black curls to a wigwam improvised with the curtains of the four-post bed in the best bedroom, Dot was sorely tried. As her eyes passed from the crown-less doll on the floor to the floss-silk ringlets hanging from the bed-furniture, her round rosy face grew rounder and rosier, and tears burst from her eyes. But in a moment more she clenched her little fists, forced back the tears, and gave vent to her favourite saying, "I don't care."

That sentence was Dot's bane and antidote; it was her vice

and her virtue. It was her standing consolation, and it brought her into all her scrapes. It was her one panacea for all the ups and downs of her life (and in the nursery where Sam developed his organ of destructiveness there were ups and downs not a few); and it was the form her naughtiness took when she was naughty.

"Don't care fell into a goose-pond, Miss Dot," said Nurse, on one occasion of the kind.

"I don't care if he did," said Miss Dot; and as Nurse knew no further feature of the goose-pond adventure which met this view of it, she closed the subject by putting Dot into the corner.

In the strength of *Don't care*, and her love for Sam, Dot bore much and long. Her dolls perished by ingenious but untimely deaths. Her toys were put to purposes for which they were never intended, and suffered accordingly. But Sam was penitent and Dot was heroic. Florinda's scalp was mended with a hot knitting-needle and a perpetual bonnet, and Dot rescued her paint-brushes from the glue-pot, and smelt her india-rubber as it boiled down in Sam's waterproof manufactory, with long-suffering forbearance.

There are, however, as we have said, limits to everything. An earthquake celebrated with the whole contents of the toy cupboard is not to be borne.

The matter was this. Early one morning Sam announced that he had a glorious project on hand. He was going to give a grand show and entertainment, far surpassing all the nursery imitations of circuses, conjurors, lectures on chemistry, and so forth, with which they had ever amused themselves. He refused to confide his plans to the faithful Dot; but he begged her to lend him all the toys she possessed, in return for which she was to be the sole spectator of the fun. He let out that the idea had suggested itself to him after the sight of a Diorama to which they had been taken, but he would not allow that it was anything of the same kind; in proof of which she was at liberty to keep back her paint-box. Dot tried hard to penetrate the secret, and to reserve some of her things from the general conscription. But Sam was obstinate. He would tell nothing, and he wanted everything. The dolls, the bricks (especially the bricks), the tea-things, the German farm, the Swiss cottages, the animals, and all the dolls' furniture. Dot gave them with a doubtful mind, and consoled herself as she watched Sam carrying pieces of board and a green table cover into the back nursery, with the prospect of the show. At last, Sam threw open the door and ushered her into the nursery rocking-chair.

The boy had certainly some constructive as well as destructive talent. Upon a sort of impromptu table covered with green cloth he had arranged all the toys in rough imitation of a town, with its streets and buildings. The relative proportion of the parts was certainly not good; but it was not Sam's fault that the doll's house and the German farm, his own brick buildings, and the Swiss cottages, were all on totally different scales of size. He had ingeniously put the larger things in the foreground, keeping the small farm-buildings from the German box at the far end of the streets, yet after all the perspective was extreme. The effect of three large horses from the toy stables in front, with the cows from the small Noah's Ark in the distance, was admirable; but the big dolls seated in an unroofed building, made with the wooden bricks on no architectural principle but that of a pound, and taking tea out of the new china tea-things, looked simply ridiculous.

Dot's eyes, however, saw no defects, and she clapped vehemently.

"Here, ladies and gentlemen," said Sam, waving his hand politely towards the rocking-chair, "you see the great city of Lisbon, the capital of Portugal—"

At this display of geographical accuracy Dot fairly cheered, and rocked herself to and fro in unmitigated enjoyment.

"—as it appeared," continued the showman, "on the morning of November 1st, 1755."

Never having had occasion to apply Mangnall's Questions to the exigencies of every-day life, this date in no way disturbed Dot's comfort.

"In this house," Sam proceeded, "a party of Portuguese ladies of rank may be seen taking tea together."

"*Breakfast*, you mean," said Dot, "you said it was in the morning, you know."

"Well, they took tea to their breakfast," said Sam. "Don't interrupt me, Dot. You are the audience, and you mustn't speak. Here you see the horses of the English ambassador out airing with his groom. There you see two peasants—no! they are *not* Noah and his wife, Dot, and if you go on talking I shall shut up. I say they are peasants peacefully driving cattle. At this moment a rumbling sound startles everyone in the city"—here Sam rolled some croquet balls up and down in a box, but the dolls sat as quiet as before, and Dot alone was startled,—"this was succeeded by a slight shock"—here he shook the table, which upset some of the buildings belonging to the German farm.—"Some houses fell."—Dot began to look anxious.—"This shock was followed by several others"—"Take care," she begged—"of increasing magnitude."—"Oh, Sam!" Dot shrieked, jumping up, "you're breaking the china!"—"The largest buildings shook to their foundations."—"Sam! Sam! the doll's house is falling," Dot cried, making wild efforts to save it: but Sam held her back with one arm, while with the other he began to pull at the boards which formed his table.—"Suddenly the ground split and opened with a fearful yawn"—Dot's shrieks shamed the impassive dolls, as Sam jerked out the boards by a dexterous movement, and doll's house, brick buildings, the farm, the Swiss cottages, and the whole toy-stock of the nursery sank together in ruins. Quite unabashed by the evident damage, Sam continued—"and in a moment the whole magnificent city of Lisbon was swallowed up. Dot! Dot! don't be a muff! What is the matter? It's splendid fun. Things must be broken some time, and I'm sure it was exactly like the real thing. Dot! why don't you speak? Dot! my dear Dot! You don't care, do you? I didn't think you'd mind it so. It was such a splendid earthquake. Oh! try not to go on like that!"

But Dot's feelings were far beyond her own control, much more that of Master Sam, at this moment. She was gasping and choking, and when at last she found breath it was only to throw herself on her face upon the floor with bitter and uncontrollable sobbing. It was certainly a mild punishment that condemned Master Sam to the back nursery for the rest of the day. It had, however, this additional severity, that during the afternoon Aunt Penelope was expected to arrive.

AUNT PENELOPE

Aunt Penelope was one of those dear, good souls who, single themselves, have, as real or adopted relatives, the interests of a dozen families, instead of one, at heart. There are few people whose youth has not owned the influence of at least one such friend. It may be a good habit, the first interest in some life-loved pursuit or favourite author, some pretty feminine art, or delicate womanly counsel enforced by those narratives of real life that are more interesting than any fiction: it may be only the periodical return of gifts and kindness, and the store of family histories that no one else can tell; but we all owe something to such an aunt or uncle—the fairy godmothers of real life.

The benefits which Sam and Dot reaped from Aunt Penelope's visits may be summed up under the heads of presents and stories, with a general leaning to indulgence in the matters of punishment, lessons, and going to bed, which perhaps is natural to aunts and uncles who have no positive responsibilities in the young people's education, and are not the daily sufferers by the lack of due discipline.

Aunt Penelope's presents were lovely. Aunt Penelope's stories were charming. There was generally a moral wrapped up in them, like the motto in a cracker-bonbon; but it was quite in the inside, so to speak, and there was abundance of smart paper and sugar-plums.

All things considered, it was certainly most proper that the much-injured Dot should be dressed out in her best, and have access to dessert, the dining-room, and Aunt Penelope, whilst Sam was kept up-stairs. And yet it was Dot who (her first burst of grief being over) fought stoutly for his pardon all the time she was being dressed, and was afterwards detected in the act of endeavouring to push fragments of raspberry tart through the nursery keyhole.

"You GOOD thing!" Sam emphatically exclaimed, as he heard her in fierce conflict on the other side of the door with the nurse who found her—"You GOOD thing! leave me alone, for I deserve it."

He really was very penitent He was too fond of Dot not to regret the unexpected degree of distress he had caused her;

and Dot made much of his penitence in her intercessions in the drawing-room.

"Sam is so very sorry," she said; "he says he knows he deserves it. I think he ought to come down. He is so *very* sorry!"

Aunt Penelope, as usual, took the lenient side, joining her entreaties to Dot's, and it ended in Master Sam's being hurriedly scrubbed and brushed, and shoved into his black velvet suit, and sent down-stairs, rather red about the eyelids, and looking very sheepish.

"Oh, Dot!" he exclaimed, as soon as he could get her into a corner, "I am so very, very sorry! particularly about the tea-things."

"Never mind," said Dot, "I don't care; and I've asked for a story, and we're going into the library." As Dot said this, she jerked her head expressively in the direction of the sofa, where Aunt Penelope was just casting on stitches preparatory to beginning a pair of her famous ribbed socks for Papa, whilst she gave to Mamma's conversation that sympathy which (like her knitting-needles) was always at the service of her large circle of friends. Dot anxiously watched the bow on the top of her cap as it danced and nodded with the force of Mamma's observations. At last it gave a little chorus of jerks, as one should say, "Certainly, undoubtedly." And then the story came to an end, and Dot, who had been slowly creeping nearer, fairly took Aunt Penelope by the hand, and carried her off, knitting and all, to the library.

"Now, please," said Dot, when she had struggled into a chair that was too tall for her.

"Stop a minute!" cried Sam, who was perched in the opposite

one, "the horse-hair tickles my legs."

"Put your pocket-handkerchief under them, as I do," said Dot. "*Now*, Aunt Penelope."

"No, wait," groaned Sam; "it isn't big enough; it only covers one leg."

Dot slid down again, and ran to Sam.

"Take my handkerchief for the other."

"But what will you do?" said Sam.

"Oh, I don't care," said Dot, scrambling back into her place. "Now, Aunty, please."

And Aunt Penelope began.

THE LAND OF LOST TOYS

"I suppose people who have children transfer their childish follies and fancies to them, and become properly sedate and grown-up. Perhaps it is because I am an old maid, and have none, that some of my nursery whims stick to me, and I find myself liking things, and wanting things, quite out of keeping with my cap and time of life. For instance. Anything in the shape of a toy-shop (from a London bazaar to a village window, with Dutch dolls, leather balls, and wooden battledores) quite unnerves me, so to speak. When I see one of those boxes containing a jar, a churn, a kettle, a pan, a coffee-pot, a cauldron on three legs, and sundry dishes, all of the smoothest wood, and with the immemorial red flower on one side of each vessel, I fairly long for an excuse for playing with them, and for trying (positively for the last

Juliana Horatia Ewing

time) if the lids *do* come off, and whether the kettle will (literally, as well as metaphorically) hold water. Then if, by good or ill luck, there is a child flattening its little nose against the window with longing eyes, my purse is soon empty; and as it toddles off with a square parcel under one arm, and a lovely being in black ringlets and white tissue paper in the other, I wish that I were worthy of being asked to join the ensuing play. Don't suppose there is any generosity in this. I have only done what we are all glad to do. I have found an excuse for indulging a pet weakness. As I said, it is not merely the new and expensive toys that attract me; I think my weakest corner is where the penny boxes lie, the wooden tea-things (with the above-named flower in miniature), the soldiers on their lazy tongs, the nine-pins, and the tiny farm.

"I need hardly say that the toy booth in a village fair tries me very hard. It tried me in childhood, when I was often short of pence, and when 'the Feast' came once a year. It never tried me more than on one occasion, lately, when I was re-visiting my old home.

"It was deep Midsummer, and the Feast. I had children with me of course (I find children, somehow, wherever I go), and when we got into the fair, there were children of people whom I had known as children, with just the same love for a monkey going up one side of a yellow stick and coming down the other, and just as strong heads for a giddy-go-round on a hot day and a diet of peppermint lozenges, as their fathers and mothers before them. There were the very same names—and here and there it seemed the very same faces—I knew so long ago. A few shillings were indeed well expended in brightening those familiar eyes: and then there were the children with me.... Besides, there really did seem to be an unusually nice assortment of things, and the man was very intelligent (in reference to his wares).... Well, well!

It was two o'clock P.M. when we went in at one end of that glittering avenue of drums, dolls, trumpets, accordions, workboxes, and what not; but what o'clock it was when I came out at the other end, with a shilling and some coppers in my pocket, and was cheered, I can't say, though I should like to have been able to be accurate about the time, because of what followed.

"I thought the best thing I could do was to get out of the fair at once, so I went up the village and struck off across some fields into a little wood that lay near. (A favourite walk in old times.) As I turned out of the booth, my foot struck against one of the yellow sticks of the climbing monkeys. The monkey was gone, and the stick broken. It set me thinking as I walked along.

"What an untold number of pretty and ingenious things one does (not wear out in honourable wear and tear, but) utterly lose, and wilfully destroy, in one's young days—things that would have given pleasure to so many more young eyes, if they had been kept a little longer—things that one would so value in later years, if some of them had survived the dissipating and destructive days of Nurserydom. I recalled a young lady I knew, whose room was adorned with knick-knacks of a kind I had often envied. They were not plaster figures, old china, wax-work flowers under glass, or ordinary ornaments of any kind. They were her old toys. Perhaps she had not had many of them, and had been the more careful of those she had. She had certainly been very fond of them, and had kept more of them than any one I ever knew. A faded doll slept in its cradle at the foot of her bed. A wooden elephant stood on the dressing-table, and a poodle that had lost his bark put out a red-flannel tongue with quixotic violence at a windmill on the opposite corner of the mantelpiece. Everything had a story of its own. Indeed the whole room must have been redolent with the sweet story of childhood, of which the toys were the illustrations, or like a poem of which the toys were the verses. She used to have children to play with them sometimes, and this was a high honour. She is married now, and has children of her own, who on birthdays and holidays will forsake the newest of their own possessions to play with 'mamma's toys.'

"I was roused from these recollections by the pleasure of getting into the wood.

"If I have a stronger predilection than my love for toys, it is my love for woods, and, like the other, it dates from childhood. It was born and bred with me, and I fancy will stay with me till I die. The soothing scents of leaf-mould, moss, and fern (not to speak of flowers)—the pale green veil in spring, the rich shade in summer, the rustle of the dry leaves in autumn, I suppose an old woman may enjoy all these, my dears, as well as you. But I think I could make 'fairy jam' of hips and haws in acorn cups now, if any child would be condescending enough to play with me. "*This* wood, too, had associations.

"I strolled on in leisurely enjoyment, and at last seated myself at the foot of a tree to rest. I was hot and tired; partly with the mid-day heat and the atmosphere of the fair, partly with the exertion of calculating change in the purchase of articles ranging in price from three farthings upwards. The tree under which I sat was an old friend. There was a hole at its base that I knew well. Two roots covered with exquisite moss ran out from each side, like the arms of a chair, and between them there accumulated year after year a rich, though tiny store of dark leaf-mould. We always used to say that fairies lived within, though I never saw anything go in myself but wood-beetles. There was one going in at that moment.

"How little the wood was changed! I bent my head for a few seconds, and, closing my eyes, drank in the delicious and suggestive scents of earth and moss about the dear old tree. I had been so long parted from the place that I could hardly believe that I was in the old familiar spot. Surely it was only one of the many dreams in which I had played again beneath those trees! But when I re-opened my eyes there was the same hole, and, oddly enough, the same beetle or one just like it. I had not noticed till that moment how much larger the hole was than it used to be in my young days.

"'I suppose the rain and so forth wears them away in time,' I said vaguely."

"'I suppose it does,' said the beetle politely; 'will you walk in?'"

"I don't know why I was not so overpoweringly astonished as you would imagine. I think I was a good deal absorbed in considering the size of the hole, and the very foolish wish that seized me to do what I had often longed to do in childhood, and creep in. I *had* so much regard for propriety as to see that there was no one to witness the escapade. Then I tucked my skirts round me, put my spectacles into my pocket for fear they should get broken, and in I went.

"I must say one thing. A wood is charming enough (no one appreciates it more than myself), but, if you have never been there, you have no idea how much nicer it is inside than on the surface. Oh, the mosses—the gorgeous mosses! The fretted lichens! The fungi like flowers for beauty, and the flowers like nothing you have ever seen!

"Where the beetle went to I don't know. I could stand up now quite well, and I wandered on till dusk in unwearied admiration. I was among some large beeches as it grew dark,

Juliana Horatia Ewing

and was beginning to wonder how I should find my way (not that I had lost it, having none to lose), when suddenly lights burst from every tree, and the whole place was illuminated. The nearest approach to this scene that I ever witnessed above ground was in a wood near the Hague in Holland. There, what look like tiny glass tumblers holding floating wicks, are fastened to the trunks of the fine old trees, at intervals of sufficient distance to make the light and shade mysterious, and to give effect to the full blaze when you reach the spot where hanging chains of lamps illuminate the 'Pavilion' and the open space where the band plays, and where the townsfolk assemble by hundreds to drink coffee and enjoy the music. I was the more reminded of the Dutch 'bosch' because, after wandering some time among the lighted trees, I heard distant sounds of music, and came at last upon a glade lit up in a similar manner, except that the whole effect was incomparably more brilliant.

"As I stood for a moment doubting whether I should proceed, and a good deal puzzled about the whole affair, I caught sight of a large spider crouched up in a corner with his stomach on the ground and his knees above his head, as some spiders do sit, and looking at me, as I fancied, through a pair of spectacles. (About the spectacles I do not feel sure. It may have been two of his bent legs in apparent connection with his prominent eyes.) I thought of the beetle, and said civilly, 'Can you tell me, sir, if this is Fairyland?' The spider took off his spectacles (or untucked his legs), and took a sideways run out of his corner.

"'Well,' he said, 'it's a Province. The fact is, it's the Land of Lost Toys. You haven't such a thing as a fly anywhere about you, have you?'"

"'No,' I said, 'I'm sorry to say I have not.' This was not strictly true, for I was not at all sorry; but I wished to be civil to the old gentleman, for he projected his eyes at me with such an intense (I had almost said greedy) gaze, that I felt quite frightened.

"'How did you pass the sentries?' he inquired."

"'I never saw any,' I answered."

"'You couldn't have seen anything if you didn't see them,' he said; 'but perhaps you don't know. They're the glow-worms. Six to each tree, so they light the road, and challenge the passers-by. Why didn't they challenge you?'"

"'I don't know,' I began, 'unless the beetle—'"

"'I don't like beetles,' interrupted the spider, stretching each leg in turn by sticking it up above him, 'all shell, and no flavour. You never tried walking on anything of that sort, did you?' and he pointed with one leg to a long thread that fastened a web above his head."

"'Certainly not,' said I."

"'I'm afraid it wouldn't bear you,' he observed slowly."

"'I'm quite sure it wouldn't,' I hastened to reply. I wouldn't try for worlds. It would spoil your pretty work in a moment. Good-evening.'"

"And I hurried forward. Once I looked back, but the spider was not following me. He was in his hole again, on his stomach, with his knees above his head, and looking (apparently through his spectacles) down the road up which I came."

"I soon forgot him in the sight before me. I had reached

Juliana Horatia Ewing

open place with the lights and the music; but how shall I describe the spectacle that I beheld?"

"I have spoken of the effect of a toy-shop on my feelings. Now imagine a toy-fair, brighter and gayer than the brightest bazaar ever seen, held in an open glade, where forest-trees stood majestically behind the glittering stalls, and stretched their gigantic arms above our heads, brilliant with a thousand hanging lamps. At the moment of my entrance all was silent and quiet. The toys lay in their places looking so incredibly attractive that I reflected with disgust that all my ready cash, except one shilling and some coppers, had melted away amid the tawdry fascinations of a village booth. I was counting the coppers (sevenpence halfpenny), when all in a moment a dozen sixpenny fiddles leaped from their places and began to play, accordions of all sizes joined them, the drumsticks beat upon the drums, the penny trumpets sounded, and the yellow flutes took up the melody on high notes, and bore it away through the trees. It was weird fairy-music, but quite delightful. The nearest approach to it that I know of above ground is to hear a wild dreamy air very well whistled to a pianoforte accompaniment.

"When the music began, all the toys rose. The dolls jumped down and began to dance. The poodles barked, the pannier donkeys wagged their ears, the wind-mills turned, the puzzles put themselves together, the bricks built houses, the balls flew from side to side, the battledores and shuttlecocks kept it up among themselves, and the skipping-ropes went round, the hoops ran off, and the sticks ran after them, the cobbler's wax at the tails of all the green frogs gave way, and they jumped at the same moment, whilst an old-fashioned go-cart ran madly about with nobody inside. It was most exhilarating.

"I soon became aware that the beetle was once more at

my elbow."

"'There are some beautiful toys here,' I said."

"'Well, yes,' he replied, 'and some odd-looking ones too. You see, whatever has been really used by any child as a plaything gets a right to come down here in the end; and there is some very queer company, I assure you. Look there.'"

"I looked, and said, 'It seems to be a potato.'"

"'So it is,' said the beetle. 'It belonged to an Irish child in one of your great cities. But to whom the child belonged I don't know, and I don't think he knew himself. He lived in the corner of a dirty, overcrowded room, and into this corner, one day, the potato rolled. It was the only plaything he ever had. He stuck two cinders into it for eyes, scraped a nose and mouth, and loved it. He sat upon it during the day, for fear it should be taken from him, but in the dark he took it out and played with it. He was often hungry, but he never ate that potato. When he died it rolled out of the corner, and was swept into the ashes. Then it came down here.'

"'What a sad story!' I exclaimed."

"The beetle seemed in no way affected."

"'It is a curious thing,' he rambled on, 'that potato takes quite a good place among the toys. You see, rank and precedence down here is entirely a question of age; that is, of the length of time that any plaything has been in the possession of a child; and all kinds of ugly old things hold the first rank; whereas the most costly and beautiful works of art have often been smashed or lost by the spoilt children of rich people in two or three days. If you care for sad stories, there is another queer thing belonging to a child who died.'"

Juliana Horatia Ewing

"It appeared to be a large sheet of canvas with some strange kind of needlework upon it."

"'It belonged to a little girl in a rich household,' the beetle continued; 'she was an invalid, and difficult to amuse. We have lots of her toys, and very pretty ones too. At last some one taught her to make caterpillars in wool-work. A bit of work was to be done in a certain stitch and then cut with scissors, which made it look like a hairy caterpillar. The child took to this, and cared for nothing else. Wool of every shade was procured for her, and she made caterpillars of all colours. Her only complaint was that they did not turn into butterflies. However, she was a sweet, gentle-tempered child, and she went on, hoping that they would do so, and making new ones. One day she was heard talking and laughing in her bed for joy. She said that all the caterpillars had become butterflies of many colours, and that the room was full of them. In that happy fancy she died.'

"And the caterpillars came down here?"

"'Not for a long time,' said the beetle; 'her mother kept them while *she* lived, and then they were lost and came down. No toys come down here till they are broken or lost.'"

"'What are those sticks doing here?' I asked."

"The music had ceased, and all the toys were lying quiet. Up in a corner leaned a large bundle of walking-sticks. They are often sold in toy-shops, but I wondered on what grounds they came here."

"'Did you ever meet with a too benevolent old gentleman wondering where on earth his sticks go to?' said the beetle. 'Why do they lend them to their grandchildren? The young rogues use them as hobby-horses and lose them, and down they come, and the sentinels cannot stop them. The real hobby-horses won't allow them to ride with them, however. There was a meeting on the subject. Every stick was put through an examination. "Where is your nose? Where is your mane? Where are your wheels?" The last was a poser. Some of them had got noses, but none of them had got wheels. So they were not true hobby-horses. Something of the kind occurred with the elder-whistles.'"

"'The what?' I asked."

"'Whistles that boys make of elder-sticks with the pith scooped out,' said the beetle. 'The real instruments would not allow them to play with them. The elder-whistles said they would not have joined had they been asked. They were amateurs, and never played with professionals. So they have private concerts with the combs and curl-papers. But, bless you, toys of this kind are endless here! Teetotums made of old cotton reels, tea-sets of acorn cups, dinner-sets of old shells, monkeys made of bits of sponge, all sorts of things made of breastbones and merrythoughts, old packs of cards that are always building themselves into houses and getting knocked down when the band begins to play, feathers, rabbits' tails—'"

"'Ah! I have heard about the rabbits' tails,' I said."

"'There they are,' the beetle continued; 'and when the band plays you will see how they skip and run. I don't believe you would find out that they had no bodies, for my experience of a warren is, that when rabbits skip and run it is the tails chiefly that you do see. But of all the amateur toys the most successful are the boats. We have a lake for our craft, you know, and there's quite a fleet of boats made out of old cork floats in fishing villages. Then, you see, the old bits of cork have really been to sea, and seen a good deal of service on the herring-nets, and so they quite take the lead of the smart shop ships, that have never been beyond a pond or a tub of water. But that's an exception. Amateur toys are mostly very dowdy. Look at that box.'"

"I looked, thought I must have seen it before, and wondered why a very common-looking box without a lid should affect me so strangely, and why my memory should seem struggling to bring it back out of the past. Suddenly it came to me—it was our old Toy Box.

"I had completely forgotten that nursery institution till recalled by the familiar aspect of the inside, which was papered with proof-sheets of some old novel on which black stars had been stamped by way of ornament. Dim memories of how these stars, and the angles of the box, and certain projecting nails interfered with the letter-press and defeated all attempts to trace the thread of the nameless narrative, stole back over my brain; and I seemed once more, with my head in the Toy Box, to beguile a wet afternoon by apoplectic endeavours to follow the fortunes of Sir Charles and Lady Belinda, as they took a favourable turn in the left-hand corner at the bottom of the trunk.

"'What are you staring at?' said the beetle."

"'It's my old Toy Box!' I exclaimed."

"The beetle rolled on to his back, and struggled helplessly with his legs: I turned him over. (Neither the first nor the last time of my showing that attention to beetles.)

"'That's right,' he said, 'set me on my legs. What a turn you gave me! You don't mean to say you have any toys here? If you have, the sooner you make your way home the better.'"

"'Why?' I inquired."

"'Well,' he said, 'there's a very strong feeling in the place. The toys think that they are ill-treated, and not taken care of by children in general. And there is some truth in it. Toys come down here by scores that have been broken the first day. And they are all quite resolved that if any of their old masters or mistresses come this way they shall be punished.'"

"'How will they be punished?' I inquired."

"Exactly as they did to their toys, their toys will do to them. All is perfectly fair and regular."

"'I don't know that I treated mine particularly badly,' I said; 'but I think I would rather go.'"

"'I think you'd better,' said the beetle. 'Good-evening!' and I saw him no more."

"I turned to go, but somehow I lost the road. At last, as I thought, I found it, and had gone a few steps when I came on a detachment of wooden soldiers, drawn up on their lazy tongs. I thought it better to wait till they got out of the way, so I turned back, and sat down in a corner in some alarm. As I did so, I heard a click, and the lid of a small box covered with mottled paper burst open, and up jumped a figure in a blue striped shirt and a rabbit-skin beard, whose eyes were intently fixed on me. He was very like my old Jack-in-a-box. My back began to creep, and I wildly meditated escape, frantically trying at the same time to recall whether it were I or my brother who originated the idea of making a small bonfire of our own one 5th of November, and burning the old Jack-in-a-box for Guy Fawkes, till nothing was left of him but a twirling bit of red-hot wire and a strong smell of frizzled fur. At this moment he nodded to me and spoke.

"'Oh! that's you, is it?' he said."

"'No, it's not,' I answered hastily; for I was quite demoralized by fear and the strangeness of the situation.

"'Who is it, then?' he inquired."

"'I'm sure I don't know,' I said; and really I was so confused that I hardly did.

"'Well, *we* know,' said the Jack-in-a-box, 'and that's all that's needed. Now, my friends,' he continued, addressing the toys who had begun to crowd round us, 'whoever recognizes a mistress and remembers a grudge—the hour of our revenge has come. Can we any of us forget the treatment we received at her hands? No! When we think of the ingenious fancy, the patient skill, that went to our manufacture; that fitted the delicate joints and springs, laid on the paint and varnish, and gave back-hair-combs and ear-rings to our smallest dolls, we feel that we deserved more care than we received. When we reflect upon the kind friends who bought us with their money, and gave us away in the benevolence of their hearts, we know that for their sakes we ought to have been longer kept and better valued. And when we remember that the sole object of our own existence was to give pleasure and amusement to our possessors, we have no hesitation in believing that we deserved a handsomer return than to have had our springs broken, our paint dirtied, and our earthly careers so untimely shortened by wilful mischief or fickle neglect. My friends, the prisoner is at the bar.'

"'I am not,' I said; for I was determined not to give in as long as resistance was possible. But as I said it I became aware, to my unutterable amazement, that I was inside the go-cart. How I got there is to this moment a mystery to me—but there I was."

"There was a great deal of excitement about the Jack-in-a-box's speech. It was evident that he was considered an orator, and, indeed, I have seen counsel in a real court look wonderfully like him. Meanwhile, my old toys appeared to be getting together. I had no idea that I had had so many. I had really been very fond of most of them, and my heart beat as the sight of them recalled scenes long forgotten, and took me back to childhood and home. There were my little gardening tools, and my slate, and there was the big doll's bedstead, that had a real mattress, and real sheets and blankets, all marked with the letter D, and a work-basket made in the blind school, and a shilling School of Art paint-box, and a wooden doll we used to call the Dowager, and innumerable other toys which I had forgotten till the sight of them recalled them to my memory, but which have again passed from my mind. Exactly opposite to me stood the Chinese mandarin, nodding as I had never seen him nod since the day when I finally stopped his performances by ill-directed efforts to discover how he did it.

"And what was that familiar figure among the rest, in a yellow silk dress and maroon velvet cloak and hood trimmed with black lace? How those clothes recalled the friends who gave them to me! And surely this was no other than my dear doll Rosa—the beloved companion of five years of my youth, whose hair I wore in a locket after I was grown up. No one could say I had ill-treated *her*. Indeed, she fixed her eyes on me with a most encouraging smile—but then she always smiled, her mouth was painted so.

"'All whom it may concern, take notice,' shouted the Jack-in-a-box, at this point, 'that the rule of this honourable court is tit for tat.'"

"'Tit, tat, tumble two,' muttered the slate in a cracked voice. (How well I remembered the fall that cracked it, and the sly games of tit tat that varied the monotony of our long multiplication sums!)

"'What are you talking about?' said the Jack-in-a-box, sharply; 'if you have grievances, state them, and you shall have satisfaction, as I told you before.'"

"'— and five make nine,' added the slate promptly, 'and six are fifteen, and eight are twenty-seven—there we go again.' I wonder why I never get up to the top of a line of figures right. It will never prove at this rate.'"

"'His mind is lost in calculations,' said the Jack-in-a-box, 'besides—between ourselves—he has been "cracky" for some time. Let some one else speak, and observe that no one is at liberty to pass a sentence on the prisoner heavier than what he has suffered from her. I reserve *my* judgment to the last.'"

"'I know what that will be,' thought I; 'oh dear! oh dear! that a respectable maiden lady should live to be burnt as a Guy Fawkes!'"

"Let the prisoner drink a gallon of iced water at once, and then be left to die of thirst."

"The horrible idea that the speaker might possibly have the power to enforce his sentence diverted my attention from the slate, and I looked round. In front of the Jack-in-a-box stood a tiny red flower-pot and saucer, in which was a miniature cactus. My thoughts flew back to a bazaar in London where, years ago, a stand of these fairy plants had excited my warmest longings, and where a benevolent old gentleman whom I had not seen before, and never saw again, bought this one and gave it to me. Vague memories of his directions for repotting and tending it reproached me from the past. My mind misgave me that after all it had died a dusty death for lack of water. True, the cactus tribe being succulent plants do not demand much moisture, but I had reason to fear that, in this instance, the principle had been applied too far, and that after copious baths of cold spring water in the first days of its popularity it had eventually perished by drought. I suppose I looked guilty, for it nodded its prickly head towards me, and said, 'Ah! you know me. You remember what I was, do you? Did you ever think of what I might have been? There was a fairy rose which came down here not long ago—a common rose enough, in a broken pot patched with string and white paint. It had lived in a street where it was the only pure beautiful thing your eyes could see. When the girl who kept it died there were eighteen roses upon it. She was eighteen years old, and they put the roses in the coffin with her when she was buried. That was worth living for. Who knows what I might have done? And what right had you to cut short a life that might have been useful?'

"Before I could think of a reply to these too just reproaches, the flower-pot enlarged, the plant shot up, putting forth new branches as it grew; then buds burst from the prickly limbs, and in a few moments there hung about it great drooping blossoms of lovely pink, with long white tassels in their throats. I had been gazing at it some time in silent and self-reproachful admiration, when I became aware that the business of this strange court was proceeding, and that the other toys were pronouncing sentence against me.

"'Tie a string round her neck and take her out bathing in the brooks,' I heard an elderly voice say in severe tones. It was the Dowager Doll. She was inflexibly wooden, and had been in the family for more than one generation."

"'It's not fair,' I exclaimed, 'the string was only to keep you from being carried away by the stream. The current is strong

Juliana Horatia Ewing

and the bank steep by the Hollow Oak Pool, and you had no arms or legs. You were old and ugly, but you would wash, and we loved you better than many waxen beauties.'

"'Old and ugly!' shrieked the Dowager. 'Tear her wig off! Scrub the paint off her face! Flatten her nose on the pavement! Saw off her legs and give her no crinoline! Take her out bathing, I say, and bring her home in a wheelbarrow with fern roots on the top of her.'"

"I was about to protest again, when the paint-box came forward, and balancing itself in an artistic, undecided kind of way on two camel's-hair brushes which seemed to serve it for feet, addressed the Jack-in-a-box."

"'Never dip your paint into the water. Never put your brush into your mouth—"

"'That's not evidence,' said the Jack-in-a-box."

"'Your notions are crude,' said the paint-box loftily; 'it's in print, and here, all of it, or words to that effect;' with which he touched the lid, as a gentleman might lay his hand upon his heart.

"'It's not evidence,' repeated the Jack-in-a-box. 'Let us proceed.'"

"'Take her to pieces and see what she's made of, if you please,' tittered a pretty German toy that moved to a tinkling musical accompaniment. 'If her works are available after that it will be an era in natural science.'"

"The idea tickled me, and I laughed."

"'Hard-hearted wretch!' growled the Dowager Doll."

"'Dip her in water and leave her to soak on a white soup-plate,' said the paint-box; 'if that doesn't soften her feelings, deprive me of my medal from the School of Art!'"

"'Give her a stiff neck!' muttered the mandarin. 'Ching Fo! give her a stiff neck.'"

"'Knock her teeth out,' growled the rake in a scratchy voice; and then the tools joined in chorus."

"'Take her out when it's fine and leave her out when it's wet, and lose her in—

"'The coal-hole,' said the spade."

"'The hay-field,' said the rake."

"'The shrubbery,' said the hoe."

"This difference of opinion produced a quarrel, which in turn seemed to affect the general behaviour of the toys, for a disturbance arose which the Jack-in-a-box vainly endeavoured to quell. A dozen voices shouted for a dozen different punishments, and (happily for me) each toy insisted upon its own wrongs being the first to be avenged, and no one would hear of the claims of any one else being attended to for an instant. Terrible sentences were passed, which I either failed to hear through the clamour then, or have forgotten now. I have a vague idea that several voices cried that I was to be sent to wash in somebody's pocket; that the work-basket wished to cram my mouth with unfinished needlework; and that through all the din the thick voice of my old leather ball monotonously repeated:

"Throw her into the dust-hole."

Juliana Horatia Ewing

"Suddenly a clear voice pierced the confusion, and Rosa tripped up."

"'My dears,' she began, 'the only chance of restoring order is to observe method. Let us follow our usual rule of precedence. I claim the first turn as the prisoner's oldest toy.'"

"'That you are not, Miss,' snapped the Dowager; 'I was in the family for fifty years.'"

"'In the family. Yes, ma'am; but you were never her doll in particular. I was her very own, and she kept me longer than any other plaything. My judgment must be first.'"

"'She is right,' said the Jack-in-a-box; 'and now let us get on. The prisoner is delivered unreservedly into the hands of our trusty and well-beloved Rosa—doll of the first class—for punishment according to the strict law of tit for tat.'"

"'I shall request the assistance of the pewter tea-things,' said Rosa, with her usual smile. 'And now, my love,' she added, turning to me, 'we will come and sit down.'"

"Where the go-cart vanished to I cannot remember, nor how I got out of it; I only know that I suddenly found myself free, and walking away with my hand in Rosa's. I remember vacantly feeling the rough edge of the stitches on her flat kid fingers, and wondering what would come next."

"'How very oddly you hold your feet, my dear,' she said; 'you stick out your toes in such an eccentric fashion, and you lean on your legs as if they were table legs, instead of supporting yourself by my hand. Turn your heels well out, and bring your toes together. You may even let them fold over each other a little; it is considered to have a pretty effect among dolls,'

"Under one of the big trees Miss Rosa made me sit down, propping me against the trunk as if I should otherwise have fallen; and in a moment more a square box of pewter tea-things came tumbling up to our feet, where the lid burst open, and all the tea-things fell out in perfect order; the cups on the saucers, the lid on the teapot, and so on.

"'Take a little tea, my love?' said Miss Rosa, pressing a pewter teacup to my lips.

"I made believe to drink, but was only conscious of inhaling a draught of air with a slight flavour of tin. In taking my second cup I was nearly choked with the teaspoon, which got into my throat.

"'What are you doing?' roared the Jack-in-a-box at this moment; 'you are not punishing her.'"

"'I am treating her as she treated me,' answered Rosa, looking as severe as her smile would allow. 'I believe that tit for tat is the rule, and that at present it is my turn.'"

"'It will be mine soon,' growled the Jack-in-a-box, and I thought of the bonfire with a shudder. However, there was no knowing what might happen before his turn did come, and meanwhile I was in friendly hands. It was not the first time my dolly and I had sat together under a tree, and, truth to say, I do not think she had any injuries to avenge."

"'When your wig comes off,' murmured Rosa, as she stole a pink kid arm tenderly round my neck, 'I'll make you a cap with blue and white rosettes, and pretend that you have had a fever.'"

"I thanked her gratefully, and was glad to reflect that I was not yet in need of an attention which I distinctly remember having shown to her in the days of her dollhood. Presently she jumped up."

"'I think you shall go to bed now, dear,' she said, and, taking my hand once more, she led me to the big doll's bedstead, which, with its pretty bed-clothes and white dimity furniture, looked tempting enough to a sleeper of suitable size. It could not have supported one quarter of my weight."

"'I have not made you a night-dress, my love,' Rosa continued; 'I am not fond of my needle, you know. *You* were not fond of your needle, I think, I fear you must go to bed in your clothes, my dear.'"

"'You are very kind,' I said, 'but I am not tired, and—it would not bear my weight.'"

"'Pooh! pooh!' said Rosa. 'My love! I remember passing one Sunday in it with the rag-doll, and the Dowager, and the Punch and Judy (the amount of pillow their two noses took up I shall never forget!), and the old doll that had nothing on, because her clothes were in the dolls' wash and did not get ironed on Saturday night, and the Highlander, whose things wouldn't come off, and who slept in his kilt. Not bear you? Nonsense! You must go to bed, my dear. I've got other things to do, and I can't leave you lying about.'"

"'The whole lot of you did not weigh one quarter of what I do,' I cried desperately. 'I cannot and will not get into that bed; I should break it all to pieces, and hurt myself into the bargain.'"

"'Well, if you will not go to bed I must put you there,' said Rosa, and without more ado, she snatched me up in her kid arms, and laid me down."

"Of course it was just as I expected. I had hardly touched the two little pillows (they had a meal-baggy smell from being stuffed with bran), when the woodwork gave way with a crash, and I fell—fell—fell—"

"Though I fully believed every bone in my body to be broken, it was really a relief to get to the ground. As soon as I could, I sat up, and felt myself all over. A little stiff, but, as it seemed, unhurt. Oddly enough, I found that I was back again under the tree; and more strange still, it was not the tree where I sat with Rosa, but the old oak-tree in the little wood. Was it all a dream? The toys had vanished, the lights were out, the mosses looked dull in the growing dusk, the evening was chilly, the hole no larger than it was thirty years ago, and when I felt in my pocket for my spectacles I found that they were on my nose.

"I have returned to the spot many times since, but I never could induce a beetle to enter into conversation on the subject, the hole remains obstinately impassable, and I have not been able to repeat my visit to the Land of Lost Toys."

"When I recall my many sins against the playthings of my childhood, I am constrained humbly to acknowledge that perhaps this is just as well."

*   *   *   *   *

SAM SETS UP SHOP

"I think you might help me, Dot," cried Sam, in dismal and rather injured tones.

It was the morning following the day of the earthquake, and of Aunt Penelope's arrival. Sam had his back to Dot, and his face to the fire, over which indeed he had bent for so long that he appeared to be half roasted.

"What do you want?" asked Dot, who was working at a doll's night-dress that had for long been partly finished, and now seemed in a fair way to completion.

"It's the glue-pot," Sam continued. "It does take so long to boil. And I have been stirring at the glue with a stick for ever so long to get it to melt. It is very hot work. I wish you would take it for a bit. It's as much for your good as for mine."

"Is it?" said Dot.

"Yes, it is, Miss," cried Sam. "You must know I've got a splendid idea."

"Not another earthquake, I hope?" said Dot, smiling.

"Now, Dot, that's truly unkind of you. I thought it was to be forgotten."

"So it is," said Dot, getting up. "I was only joking. What is the idea?"

"I don't think I shall tell you till I have finished my shop. I want to get to it now, and I wish you would take a turn at the glue-pot."

Sam was apt to want a change of occupation. Dot, on the other hand, was equally averse from leaving what she was about till it was finished, so they suited each other like Jack Sprat and his wife. It had been an effort to Dot to leave the night-dress which she had hoped to finish at a sitting; but when she was fairly set to work on the glue business she never moved till the glue was in working order, and her face as red as a ripe tomato.

By this time Sam had set up business in the window-seat, and was fastening a large paper inscription over his shop. It ran thus:—

*   *   *   *   *

MR. SAM.

Dolls' Doctor and Toymender to Her Majesty the Queen, and all other Potentates.

*   *   *   *   *

"Splendid!" shouted Dot, who was serving up the glue as if it had been a kettle of soup, and who looked herself very like an over-toasted cook.

Sam took the glue, and began to bustle about.

"Now, Dot, get me all the broken toys, and we'll see what we can do. And here's a second splendid idea. Do you see that box? Into that we shall put all the toys that are quite spoiled and cannot possibly be mended. It is to be called the Hospital for Incurables. I've got a placard for that. At least it's not written yet, but here's the paper, and perhaps you would write it, Dot, for I am tired of writing, and I want to begin the mending."

"For the future," he presently resumed, "when I want a doll to scalp or behead, I shall apply to the Hospital for Incurables, and the same with any other toy that I want to destroy. And you will see, my dear Dot, that I shall be quite a blessing to the nursery; for I shall attend the dolls gratis, and

Juliana Horatia Ewing

keep all the furniture in repair."

Sam really kept his word. He had a natural turn for mechanical work, and, backed by Dot's more methodical genius, he prolonged the days of the broken toys by skilful mending, and so acquired an interest in them which was still more favourable to their preservation. When his birthday came round, which was some months after these events, Dot (assisted by Mamma and Aunt Penelope) had prepared for him a surprise that was more than equal to any of his own "splendid ideas." The whole force of the toy cupboard was assembled on the nursery table, to present Sam with a fine box of joiner's tools as a reward for his services, Papa kindly acting as spokesman on the occasion.

And certain gaps in the china tea-set, some scars on the dolls' faces, and a good many new legs, both amongst the furniture and the animals, are now the only remaining traces of Sam's earthquake.

*   *   *   *   *

THREE CHRISTMAS TREES

This is a story of Three Christmas Trees. The first was a real one, but the child we are to speak of did not see it. He saw the other two, but they were not real; they only existed in his fancy. The plot of the story is very simple; and, as it has been described so early, it is easy for those who think it stupid to lay the book down in good time.

Probably every child who reads this has seen one Christmas tree or more; but in the small town of a distant colony with which we have to do, this could not at one time have been said. Christmas-trees were then by no means so universal, even in England, as they now are, and in this little colonial town they were unknown. Unknown, that is, till the Governor's wife gave her great children's party. At which point we will begin the story.

The Governor had given a great many parties in his time. He had entertained big wigs and little wigs, the passing military, and the local grandees. Everybody who had the remotest claim to attention had been attended to: the ladies had had their full share of balls and pleasure parties: only one class of the population had any complaint to prefer against his hospitality; but the class was a large one—it was the children. However, he, was a bachelor, and knew little or nothing about little boys and girls: let us pity rather than blame him.

At last he took to himself a wife; and among the many advantages of this important step, was a due recognition of the claims of these young citizens. It was towards happy Christmas-tide that "the Governor's amiable and admired lady" (as she was styled in the local newspaper) sent out notes for her first children's party. At the top of the note-paper was a very red robin, who carried a blue Christmas greeting in his mouth, and at the bottom—written with A.D.C.'s best flourish—were the magic words, *A Christmas Tree*. In spite of the flourishes—partly perhaps because of them—the A.D.C.'s handwriting, though handsome, was rather illegible. But for all this, most of the children invited contrived to read these words, and those who could not do so were not slow to learn the news by hearsay. There was to be a Christmas Tree! It would be like a birthday party, with this above ordinary birthdays, that there were to be presents for every one. One of the children invited lived in a little white house, with a spruce fir-tree before the door. The spruce fir did this good service to the little house, that it helped people to find their way to it; and it was by no means easy for a stranger to find his way to any given house in this little town, especially if the house were small and white, and stood in one of the back streets. For most of the houses were small, and most of them were painted white, and back streets ran parallel with each other, and had no names, and were all so much alike that it was very confusing. For instance, if you had asked the way to Mr. So-and-So's, it is very probable that some friend would have directed you as follows: "Go straight forward and take the first turning to your left, and you will find that there are four streets, which run at right angles to the one you are in, and parallel with each other. Each of them has got a big pine in it—one of the old forest trees. Take the last street but one, and the fifth white house you come to is Mr. So-and-So's. He has green blinds and a coloured servant." You would not always have got such clear directions as these, but with them you would probably have found the house at last, partly by accident, partly by the blinds and coloured servant. Some of the neighbours affirmed that the little white house had a name; that all the houses and streets had names, only they were traditional and not recorded anywhere; that very few people knew them, and nobody made any use of them. The name of the little white house was said to be Trafalgar Villa, which seemed so inappropriate to the modest peaceful little home, that the man who lived in it tried to find out why it had been so called. He thought that his predecessor must have been in the navy, until he found that he had been the owner of what is called a "dry-goods store," which seems to mean a shop where things are sold which are not good to eat or drink— such as drapery. At last somebody said, that as there was a public-house called the "Duke of Wellington" at the corner of the street, there probably had been a nearer one called "The Nelson," which had been burnt down, and that the man who built "The Nelson" had built the house with the spruce fir before it, and that so the name had arisen. An explanation which was just so far probable, that public-houses and fires were of frequent occurrence in those parts.

But this has nothing to do with the story. Only we must say, as we said before, and as we should have said had we been living there then, the child we speak of lived in the little white house with one spruce fir just in front of it.

Of all the children who looked forward to the Christmas tree, he looked forward to it the most intensely. He was an imaginative child, of a simple, happy nature, easy to please. His father was an Englishman, and in the long winter evenings he would tell the child tales of the old country, to which his mother would listen also. Perhaps the parents enjoyed these stories the most. To the boy they were new, and conesquently delightful, but to the parents they were old; and as regards some stories, that is better still.

"What kind of a bird is this on my letter?" asked the boy on the day which brought the Governor's lady's note of invitation. "And oh! what is a Christmas tree?"

"The bird is an English robin," said his father. "It is quite another bird to that which is called a robin here: it is smaller and rounder, and has a redder breast and bright dark eyes, and lives and sings at home through the winter. A Christmas tree is a fir-tree—just such a one as that outside the door—brought into the house and covered with lights and presents. Picture to yourself our fir-tree lighted up with tapers on all the branches, with dolls, and trumpets, and bon-bons, and drums, and toys of all kinds hanging from it like fir-cones, and on the tip-top shoot a figure of a Christmas Angel in white, with a star upon its head."

"Fancy!" said the boy.

And fancy he did. Every day he looked at the spruce fir, and tried to imagine it laden with presents, and brilliant with tapers, and thought how wonderful must be that "old country"—*Home*, as it was called, even by those who had never seen it—where the robins were so very red, and where at Christmas the fir-trees were hung with toys instead of cones.

It was certainly a pity that, two days before the party, an original idea on the subject of snowmen struck one of the children who used to play together, with their sleds and snow shoes, in the back streets. The idea was this: That instead of having a commonplace snowman, whose legs were obliged to be mere stumps, for fear he should be top-heavy, and who could not walk, even with them; who, in fact, could do nothing but stand at the corner of the street, holding his impotent stick, and staring with his pebble eyes, till he was broken to pieces or ignominiously carried away by a thaw,—

that, instead of this, they should have a real, live snowman, who should walk on competent legs, to the astonishment, and (happy thought!) perhaps to the alarm of the passers-by. This delightful novelty was to be accomplished by covering one of the boys of the party with snow till he looked as like a real snowman as circumstances would admit. At first everybody wanted to be the snowman, but, when it came to the point, it was found to be so much duller to stand still and be covered up than to run about and work, that no one was willing to act the part. At last it was undertaken by the little boy from the Fir House. He was somewhat small, but then he was so good-natured he would always do as he was asked. So he stood manfully still, with his arms folded over a walking-stick upon his breast, whilst the others heaped the snow upon him. The plan was not so successful as they had hoped. The snow would not stick anywhere except on his shoulders, and when it got into his neck he cried with the cold; but they were so anxious to carry out their project, that they begged him to bear it "just a little longer"; and the urchin who had devised the original idea wiped the child's eyes with his handkerchief, and (with that hopefulness which is so easy over other people's matters) "dared say that when all the snow was on, he wouldn't feel it." However, he did feel it, and that so severely that the children were obliged to give up the game, and, taking the stick out of his stiff little arms, to lead him home.

It appears that it is with snowmen as with some other men in conspicuous positions. It is easier to find fault with them than to fill their place.

The end of this was a feverish cold, and, when the day of the party came, the ex-snowman was still in bed. It is due to the other children to say that they felt the disappointment as keenly as he did, and that it greatly damped the pleasure of the party for them to think that they had prevented his

Juliana Horatia Ewing

sharing in the treat. The most penitent of all was the deviser of the original idea. He had generously offered to stay at home with the little patient, which was as generously refused; but the next evening he was allowed to come and sit on his bed, and describe it all for the amusement of his friend. He was a quaint boy, this urchin, with a face as broad as an American Indian's, eyes as bright as a squirrel's, and all the mischief in life lurking about him, till you could see roguishness in the very folds of his hooded Indian winter coat of blue and scarlet. In his hand he brought the sick child's present: a dray with two white horses, and little barrels that took off and on, and a driver, with wooden joints, a cloth coat, and everything, in fact, that was suitable to the driver of a brewer's dray, except that he had blue boots and earrings, and that his hair was painted in braids like a lady's, which is clearly the fault of the doll manufacturers, who will persist in making them all of the weaker sex.

"And what was the Christmas tree like?" asked the invalid.

"Exactly like the fir outside your door," was the reply. "Just about that size, and planted in a pot covered with red cloth. It was kept in another room till after tea, and then when the door was opened it was like a street fire in the town at night—such a blaze of light—candles everywhere! And on all the branches the most beautiful presents. I got a drum and a penwiper."

"Was there an angel?" the child asked.

"Oh, yes!" the boy answered. "It was on the tip-top branch, and it was given to me, and I brought it for you, if you would like it; for, you know, I am so very, very sorry I thought of a snowman and made you ill, and I do love you, and beg you to forgive me."

And the roguish face stooped over the pillow to be kissed; and out of a pocket in the hooded coat came forth the Christmas Angel. In the face it bore a strong family likeness to the drayman, but its feet were hidden in folds of snowy muslin, and on its head glittered a tinsel star.

"How lovely!" said the child. "Father told me about this. I like it best of all. And it is very kind of you, for it is not your fault that I caught cold. I should have liked it if we could have done it, but I think to enjoy being a snowman, one should be snow all through."

They had tea together, and then the invalid was tucked up for the night. The dray was put away in the cupboard, but he took the angel to bed with him.

And so ended the first of the Three Christmas Trees.

* * * * *

Except for a warm glow from the wood fire in the stove, the room was dark; but about midnight it seemed to the child that a sudden blaze of light filled the chamber. At the same moment the window curtains were drawn aside, and he saw that the spruce fir had come close up to the panes and was peeping in. Ah! how beautiful it looked! It had become a Christmas tree. Lighted tapers shone from every familiar branch, toys of the most fascinating appearance hung like fruit, and on the tip-top shoot there stood the Christmas Angel. He tried to count the candles, but somehow it was impossible. When he looked at them they seemed to change places—to move—to become like the angel, and then to be candles again, whilst the flames nodded to each other and repeated the blue greeting of the robin, "A Merry Christmas and a Happy New Year!" Then he tried to distinguish the presents, but, beautiful as the toys looked, he could not

Juliana Horatia Ewing

exactly discover what any of them were, or choose which he would like best. Only the Angel he could see clearly—so clearly! It was more beautiful than the doll under his pillow; it had a lovely face like his own mother's, he thought, and on its head gleamed a star far brighter than tinsel. Its white robes waved with the flames of the tapers, and it stretched its arms towards him with a smile.

"I am to go and choose my present," thought the child; and he called "Mother! Mother dear! please open the window."

But his mother did not answer. So he thought he must get up himself, and with an effort he struggled out of bed.

But when he was on his feet, everything seemed changed! Only the firelight shone upon the walls, and the curtains were once more firmly closed before the window. It had been a dream, but so vivid that in his feverish state he still thought it must be true, and dragged the curtains back to let in the glorious sight again. The firelight shone upon a thick coating of frost upon the panes, but no further could he see, so with all his strength he pushed the window open and leaned out into the night.

The spruce fir stood in its old place; but it looked very beautiful in its Christmas dress. Beneath it lay a carpet of pure white. The snow was clustered in exquisite shapes upon its plumy branches; wrapping the tree top with its little cross shoots, as a white robe might wrap a figure with outstretched arms.

There were no tapers to be seen, but northern lights shot up into the dark blue sky, and just over the fir-tree shone a bright, bright star.

"Jupiter looks well to-night," said the old Professor in the town observatory, as he fixed his telescope; but to the child it seemed as the star of the Christmas Angel.

His mother had really heard him call, and now came and put him back to bed again. And so ended the second of the Three Christmas Trees.

*   *   *   *   *

It was enough to have killed him, all his friends said; but it did not. He lived to be a man, and—what is rarer—to keep the faith, the simplicity, the tender-heartedness, the vivid fancy of his childhood. He lived to see many Christmas trees "at home," in that old country where the robins are red-breasts, and sing in winter. There a heart as good and gentle as his own became one with his; and once he brought his young wife across the sea to visit the place where he was born. They stood near the little white house, and he told her the story of the Christmas trees.

"This was when I was a child," he added.

"But that you are still," said she; and she plucked a bit of the fir-tree and kissed it, and carried it away.

He lived to tell the story to his children, and even to his grandchildren; but he never was able to decide which of the two was the more beautiful—the Christmas Tree of his dream, or the Spruce Fir as it stood in the loveliness of that winter night.

This is told, not that it has anything to do with any of the Three Christmas Trees, but to show that the story is a happy one, as is right and proper; that the hero lived, and married, and had children, and was as prosperous as good people, in books, should always be.

Juliana Horatia Ewing

Of course he died at last. The best and happiest of men must die; and it is only because some stories stop short in their history, that every hero is not duly buried before we lay down the book.

When death came for our hero he was an old man. The beloved wife, some of his children, and many of his friends had died before him, and of those whom he had loved there were fewer to leave than to rejoin. He had had a short illness, with little pain, and was now lying on his deathbed in one of the big towns in the North of England. His youngest son, a clergy-man, was with him, and one or two others of his children, and by the fire sat the doctor.

The doctor had been sitting by the patient, but now that he could do no more for him he had moved to the fire; and they had taken the ghastly, half-emptied medicine bottles from the table by the bedside, and had spread it with a fair linen cloth, and had set out the silver vessels of the Supper of the Lord. The old man had been "wandering" somewhat during the day. He had talked much of going home to the old country, and with the wide range of dying thoughts he had seemed to mingle memories of childhood with his hopes of Paradise. At intervals he was clear and collected—one of those moments had been chosen for his last sacrament—and he had fallen asleep with the blessing in his ears.

He slept so long and so peacefully that the son almost began to hope that there might be a change, and looked towards the doctor, who still sat by the fire with his right leg crossed over his left. The doctor's eyes were also on the bed, but at that moment he drew out his watch and looked at it with an air of professional conviction, which said, "It's only a question of time." Then he crossed his left leg over his right, and turned to the fire again. Before the right leg should be tired, all would be over. The son saw it as clearly as if it had been spoken, and he too turned away and sighed.

As they sat, the bells of a church in the town began to chime for midnight service, for it was Christmas Eve, but they did not wake the dying man. He slept on and on.

The doctor dozed. The son read in the Prayer Book on the table, and one of his sisters read with him. Another, from grief and weariness, slept with her head upon his shoulder. Except for a warm glow from the fire, the room was dark. Suddenly the old man sat up in bed, and, in a strong voice, cried with inexpressible enthusiasm,

"*How beautiful!*"

The son held back his sisters, and asked quietly,

"*What*, my dear Father?"

"The Christmas Tree!" he said in a low, eager voice. "Draw back the curtains."

They were drawn back; but nothing could be seen, and still the old man gazed as if in ecstasy.

"Light!" he murmured. "The Angel! the Star!"

Again there was silence; and then he stretched forth his hands, and cried passionately,

"The Angel is beckoning to me! Mother! Mother dear! Please open the window."

The sash was thrown open, and all eyes turned involuntarily where those of the dying man were gazing. There was no Christmas tree—no tree at all. But over the house-tops the

Juliana Horatia Ewing

morning star looked pure and pale in the dawn of Christmas Day. For the night was past, and above the distant hum of the streets the clear voices of some waits made the words of an old carol heard—words dearer for their association than their poetry:

"While shepherds watched their flocks by night,
All seated on the ground,
The Angel of the Lord came down,
And glory shone around."

When the window was opened, the soul passed; and when they looked back to the bed the old man had lain down again, and, like a child, was smiling in his sleep—his last sleep.

And this was the Third Christmas Tree.

*   *   *   *   *

AN IDYLL OF THE WOOD

"Tell us a story," said the children, "a sad one, if you please, and a little true. But, above all, let it end badly, for we are tired of people who live happily ever after."

"I heard one lately," said the old man who lived in the wood; "it is founded on fact, and is a sad one also; but whether it ends badly or no I cannot pretend to say. That is a matter of taste: what is a bad ending?"

"A story ends badly," said the children with authority, "when people die, and nobody marries anybody else, especially if it is a prince and princess."

"A most lucid explanation," said the old man. "I think my story will do, for the principal character dies, and there is no wedding."

"Tell it, tell it!" cried his hearers, "and tell us also where you got it from."

"Who knows the riches of a wood in summer?" said the old man. "In summer, do I say? In spring, in autumn, or in winter either. Who knows them? You, my children? Well, well. Better than some of your elders, perchance. You know the wood where I live; the hollow tree that will hold five children, and Queen Mab knows how many fairies. (What a castle it makes! And if it had but another floor put into it, with a sloping ladder—like one of the round towers of Ireland—what a house for children to live in! With no room for lesson-books, grown-up people, or beds!)

"You know the way to the hazel copse, and the place where the wild strawberries grow. You know where the wren sits on her eggs, and, like good children, pass by with soft steps and hushed voices, that you may not disturb that little mother. You know (for I have shown you) where the rare fern grows—a habitat happily yet unnoted in scientific pages. *We* never add its lovely fronds to our nosegays, and if we move a root it is but to plant it in another part of the wood, with as much mystery and circumspection as if we were performing some solemn druidical rite. It is to us as a king in hiding, and the places of its abode we keep faithfully secret. It will be thus held sacred by us until, with all the seed its untouched fronds have scattered, and all the offshoots we have propagated, it shall have become as plentiful as Heaven intends all beautiful things to be. Every one is not so scrupulous. There are certain ladies and gentlemen who picnic near my cottage in the hot weather, and who tell each other that they love a wood. Most of these good people have nevertheless neither eyes nor ears for what goes on around them, except that they hear each other, and see the cold collation. They will picnic there summer after summer, and not know whether they sit under oaks or ashes, beeches or elms. All birds sing for them the same song. Tell *them* that such a plant is rare in the neighbourhood, that there are but few specimens of it, and it will not long be their fault if there are any. Does any one direct them to it, they tear it ruthlessly up and carry it away. If by any chance a root is left, it is left so dragged and pulled and denuded of earth, that there is small chance that it will survive. Probably, also, the ravished clump dies in the garden or pot to which it is transplanted, either from neglect, or from ignorance of the conditions essential to its life; and the rare plant becomes yet rarer. Oh! without doubt they love a wood. It gives more shade than the largest umbrella, and is cheaper for summer entertainment than a tent: there you get canopy and carpet, fuel and water, shade and song, and beauty—all gratis; and these are not small matters when one has invited a large party of one's acquaintance. There are insects, it is true, which somewhat disturb our friends; and as they do not know which sting, and which are harmless, they kill all that come within their reach, as a safe general principle. The town boys, too! They know the wood—that is to say, they know where the wild fruits grow, and how to chase the squirrel, and rob the birds' nests, and snare the birds. Well, well, my children; to know and love a wood truly, it may be that one must live in it as I have done; and then a lifetime will scarcely reveal all its beauties, or exhaust its lessons. But even then, one must have eyes that see, and ears that hear, or one misses a good deal. It was in the wood that I heard this story that I shall tell you."

"How did you hear it?" asked the children.

"A thrush sang it to me one night."

"One night?" said the children. "Then you mean a nightingale."

"I mean a thrush," said the old man. "Do I not know the note of one bird from another? I tell you that pine-tree by my cottage has a legend of its own, and the topmost branch is haunted. Must all legends be about the loves and sorrows of our self-satisfied race alone?"

"But did you really and truly hear it?" they asked. "I heard it," said the old man. "But, as I tell you, one hears and one hears. I don't say that everybody would have heard it, merely by sleeping in my chamber; but, for the benefit of the least imaginative, I will assure you that it is founded on fact."

"Begin! begin!" shouted the children.

"Once upon a time," said the old man, "there was a young thrush, who was born in that beautiful dingle where we last planted the—fern. His home-nest was close to the ground, but the lower one is, the less fear of falling; and in woods, the elevation at which you sleep is a matter of taste, and not of expense or gentility. He awoke to life when the wood was dressed in the pale fresh green of early summer; and believing, like other folk, that his own home was at least the principal part of the world, earth seemed to him so happy and so beautiful an abode, that his heart felt ready to burst with joy. The ecstasy was almost pain, till wings and a voice came to him. Then, one day, when, after a grey morning, the sun came out at noon, drawing the scent from the old pine that looks in at my bedroom window, his joy burst forth, after long silence, into song, and flying upwards, he sat on the topmost branch of the pine, and sang as loud as he could sing to the sun and the blue sky.

"'Joy! joy!' he sang. 'Fresh water and green woods, ambrosial sunshine and sunflecked shade, chattering brooks and rustling leaves, glade, and sward, and dell. Lichens and cool mosses, feathered ferns and flowers. Green leaves! Green leaves! Summer! summer! summer!'

"It was monotonous, but every word came from the singer's heart, which is not always the case. Thenceforward, though he slept near the ground, he went up every day to this pine, as to some sacred high place, and sang the same song, of which neither he nor I were ever weary.

"Let one be ever so inoffensive, however, one is not long left in peace in this world, even in a wood. The thrush sang too loudly of his simple happiness, and some boys from the town heard him and snared him, and took him away in a dirty cloth cap, where he was nearly smothered. The world is certainly not exclusively composed of sunshine, and green woods, and odorous pines. He became almost senseless during the hot dusty walk that led to the town. It was a seaport town, about two miles from the wood, a town of narrow, steep streets, picturesque old houses, and odours compounded of tar, dead fish, and many other scents less agreeable than forest perfumes. The thrush was put into a small wicker-cage in an upper room, in one of the narrowest and steepest of the streets. "'I shall die to-night,' he piped. But he did not. He lived that night, and for several nights and days following. The boys took small care of him, however. He was often left without food, without water, and always with too little air. Two or three times they tried to sell him, but he was not bought, for no one could hear him sing. One day he was hung outside the window, and partly owing to the sun and fresh air, and partly because a woman was singing in the street, he began to carol his old song.

"The woman was a street singer. She was even paler, thinner, and more destitute-looking than such women usually are. In some past time there had been beauty and feeling in her face, but the traces of both were well-nigh gone. An indifference almost amounting to vacancy was there now, and, except that she sang, you might almost have fancied her a corpse. In her voice, also, there had once been beauty and feeling, and here again the traces were small indeed. From time to time, she was stopped by fits of coughing, when an ill-favoured hunchback, who accompanied her on a tambourine, swore and scowled at her. She sang a song of sentiment, with a refrain about

'Love and truth,

Juliana Horatia Ewing

And joys of youth—'

on which the melody dwelt and quavered as if in mockery. As she sang, a sailor came down the street. His collar was very large, his trousers were very wide, his hat hung on the back of his head more as an ornament than for shelter; and he had one of the roughest faces and the gentlest hearts that ever went together since Beauty was entertained by the Beast. His hands were in his pockets, where he could feel one shilling and a penny, all the spare cash that remained to him after a friendly stroll through the town. When he saw the street singer, he stopped, pulled off his hat, and scratched his head, as was his custom when he was puzzled or interested.

"'It's no good keeping an odd penny,' he said to himself; 'poor thing, she looks bad enough!' And, bringing the penny to the surface out of the depths of his pocket, he gave it to the woman. The hunchback came forward to take it, but the sailor passed him with a shove of his elbow, and gave it to the singer, who handed it over to her companion without moving a feature, and went on with her song."

"'I'd like to break every bone in your ugly body,' muttered the sailor, with a glance at the hunchback, who scowled in return."

"'I shall die of this close street, and of all I have suffered,' thought the thrush."

"'Green leaves! green leaves!' he sang, for it was the only song he knew."

"'My voice is gone,' thought the hunchback's companion. 'He'll beat me again to-night; but it can't last long:

"Love and truth,

And joys of youth—"

she sang, for that was the song she had learned; and it was not her fault that it was inappropriate.

"But the ballad-singer's captivity was nearly at an end. When the hunchback left her that evening to spend the sailor's penny with the few others which she had earned, he swore that when he came back he would make her sing louder than she had done all day. Her face showed no emotion, less than it did when he saw it hours after, when beauty and feeling seemed to have returned to it in the peace of death, when he came back and found the cage empty, and that the long-prisoned spirit had flown away to seek the face of love and truth indeed."

"But how about the thrush?"

"The sailor had scarcely swallowed the wrath which the hunchback had stirred in him, when his ear was caught by the song of the thrush above him."

"'You sing uncommon well, pretty one,' he said, stopping and putting his hat even farther back than usual to look up. He was one of those good people who stop a dozen times in one street, and look at everything as they go along; whereby you may see three times as much of life as other folk, but it is a terrible temptation to spend money. It was so in this instance. The sailor looked till his kindly eye perceived that the bird was ill-cared for."

"'It should have a bit of sod, it *should*,' he said emphatically, taking his hat off, and scratching his head again; 'and there's not a crumb of food on board. Maybe, they don't understand the ways of birds here. It would be a good turn to mention it.'"

Juliana Horatia Ewing

"With this charitable intention he entered the house, and when he left it, his pocket was empty, and the thrush was carried tenderly in his handkerchief."

"'The canary died last voyage,' he muttered apologetically to himself, 'and the money always does go somehow or other.'"

"The sailor's hands were about three times as large and coarse as those of the boy who had carried the thrush before, but they seemed to him three times more light and tender— they were handy and kind, and this goes farther than taper fingers."

"The thrush's new home was not in the narrow streets. It was in a small cottage in a small garden at the back of the town. The canary's old cage was comparatively roomy, and food, water, and fresh turf were regularly supplied to him. He could see green leaves too. There was an apple-tree in the garden, and two geraniums, a fuchsia, and a tea-rose in the window. Near the tea-rose an old woman sat in the sunshine. She was the sailor's mother, and looked very like a tidily-kept window-plant herself. She had a little money of her own, which gave her a certain dignity, and her son was very good to her; and so she dwelt in considerable comfort, dividing her time chiefly between reading in the big Bible, knitting socks for Jack, and raising cuttings in bottles of water. She had heard of hothouses and forcing-frames, but she did not think much of them. She believed a bottle of water to be the most natural, because it was the oldest method she knew of, and she thought no good came of new-fangled ways, and trying to outdo Nature."

"'Slow and sure is best,' she said, and stuck to her own system."

"'What's that, my dear?' she asked, when the sailor came in

and held up the handkerchief. He told her."

"'You're always a-laying out your money on something or other,' said the old lady, who took the privilege of her years to be a little testy. 'What did you give for *that*?'"

"A shilling, ma'am."

"'Tst! tst! tst!' said the old lady, disapprovingly."

"'Now, Mother, don't shake that cap of yours off your head,' said the sailor. 'What's a shilling? If I hadn't spent it, I should have changed it; and once change a shilling, and it all dribbles away in coppers, and you get nothing for it. But spend it in the lump, and you get something you want. That's what I say.'"

"'*I* want no more pets,' said the old lady, stiffly."

"'Well, you won't be troubled with this one long,' said her son; 'it'll go with me, and that's soon enough.'"

"Any allusion to his departure always melted the old lady, as Jack well knew. She became tearful, and begged him to leave the thrush with her."

"'You know, my dear, I've always looked to your live things as if they were Christians; and loved them too (unless it was that monkey that I never *could* do with!). Leave it with me, my dear. I'd never bother myself with a bird on board ship, if I was you.'

"'That's because you've got a handsome son of your own, old lady,' chuckled the sailor; 'I've neither chick nor child, ma'am, remember, and a man must have something to look to. The bird'll go with me.'"

Juliana Horatia Ewing

"And so it came to pass that just when the thrush was becoming domesticated, and almost happy at the cottage, one morning the sailor brought him fresh turf and groundsel, besides his meal-cake, and took the cage down. And the old woman kissed the wires, and bade the bird good-bye, and blessed her son, and prayed Heaven to bring him safe home again; and they went their way."

"The forecastle of a steam-ship (even of a big one) is a poor exchange for a snug cottage to any one but a sailor. To Jack, the ship was home. *He* had never lived in a wood, and carolled in tree-tops. He preferred blue to green, and pine masts to pine trees; and he smoked his pipe very comfortably in the forecastle, whilst the ship rolled to and fro, and swung the bird's cage above his head. To the thrush it was only an imprisonment that grew worse as time went on. Each succeeding day made him pine more bitterly for his native woods—for fresh air and green leaves, and the rest and quiet, and sweet perfumes, and pleasant sounds of country life. His turf dried up, his groundsel withered, and no more could be got. He longed even to be back with the old woman—to see the apple-tree, and the window-plants, and be still. The shudder of the screw, the blasts of hot air from the engine and cook's galley, the ceaseless jangling, clanging, pumping noises, and all the indescribable smells which haunt a steam-ship, became more wearisome day by day. Even when the cage was hung outside, the, sea breeze seemed to mock him with its freshness. The rich blue of the waters gave him no pleasure, his eyes failed with looking for green, the bitter, salt spray vexed him, and the wind often chilled him to the bone, whilst the sun shone, and icebergs gleamed upon the horizon.

"The sailor had been so kind a master, that the thrush had become deeply attached to him, as birds will; and while at the cottage he had scarcely fretted after his beloved wood.

But with every hour of the voyage, home-sickness came more strongly upon him, and his heart went back to the nest, and the pine-top, and the old home. When one sleeps soundly, it is seldom that one remembers one's dreams; but when one is apt to be roused by an unexpected lurch of the ship, by the moan of a fog-whistle, or the scream of an engine, one becomes a light sleeper, and the visions of the night have a strange reality, and are easily recalled. And now the thrush always dreamt of home.

"One day he was hung outside. It was not a very fine day, but he looked drooping, and the pitying sailor brought him out, to get some air. His heart was sore with home-sickness, and he watched the sea-birds skimming up and down with envious eyes. It seemed all very well for poor men, who hadn't so much as a wing to carry them over the water, to build lumbering sea-nests, with bodies to float in the water like fish, and wings of canvas to carry them along, and to help it out with noisy steam-engines—and to endure it all. But for him, who could fly over a hundred tree-tops before a man could climb to one, it was hard to swing outside a ship, and to watch other birds use their wings, when his, which quivered to fly homewards, could only flutter against the bars. As he thought, a roll of the ship threw him forward, the wind shook the wires of the cage, and loosened the fastening; and, when the vessel righted, the cage-door swung slowly open.

"At this moment, a ray of sunshine streaked the deep blue water, and a gleaming sea bird, which had been sitting like a tuft of foam upon a wave, rose with outstretched pinions, and soared away. It was too much. With one shrill pipe of hope, the thrush fluttered from his cage, spread his wings, and followed him."

"When the sailor found that the wind was getting up, he

came to take the cage down, and then his grief was sore indeed."

"'The canary died last voyage,' he said, sadly. 'The cage was bought on a Friday, and I knew ill luck would come of it. I said so to Mother; but the old lady says there's no such thing as luck, and she's Bible-learned, if ever a woman was. "That's very true," says I, "but if I'd the money for another cage, I wouldn't use this;" and I never will again. Poor, bird! it was a sweet singer.' And he turned his face aside."

"'It may have the sense to come back,' said one of the crew. The sailor scratched his head, and shook it sadly."

"'Noah's bird came back to him, when she found no rest,' he said, 'but I don't think mine will, Tom.'"

"He was right. The thrush returned no more. He did not know how wide was the difference between his own strength and that of the bird he followed. The sea-fowl cut the air with wings of tenfold power: he swooped up and down, he stooped to fish, he rested on the ridges of the dancing waves, and then, with one steady flight, he disappeared, and the thrush was left alone. Other birds passed him, and flew about him, and fished, and rocked upon the waters near him, but he held steadily on. Ships passed him also, but too far away for him to rest upon; whales spouted in the distance, and strange fowl screamed; but not a familiar object broke the expanse of the cold sea. He did not know what course he was taking. He hoped against hope that he was going home. Although he was more faint and weary than he had ever yet been, he felt no pain. The intensity of his hope to reach the old wood made everything seem light; even at the last, when his wings were almost powerless, he believed that they would bear him home, and was happy. Already he seemed to rest upon the trees, the waters sounded in his ears like the rustling of leaves, and the familiar scent of the pine-tree seemed to him to come upon the breeze.

"In this he was not wrong. A country of pine-woods was near; and land was in sight, though too far away for him to reach it now. Not home, but yet a land of wondrous summer beauty; of woods, and flowers, and sun-flecked leaves—of sunshine more glowing than he had ever known—of larger ferns, and deeper mosses, and clearer skies—a land, of balmy summer nights, where the stars shine brighter than with us, and where fireflies appear and vanish, like stars of a lower firmament, amid the trees. As the sun broke out, the scent of pines came strong upon the land breeze. A strange land, but the thrush thought it was his own.

"'I smell woods,' he chirped faintly; 'I see the sun. This is home!'"

"All round him, the noisy crests of the fresh waves seemed to carol the song he could no longer sing—'Home, home! fresh water and green woods, ambrosial sunshine and sun-flecked shade, chattering brooks and rustling leaves, glade and sward and dell, lichens and cool mosses, feathered ferns and flowers. Green leaves! green leaves! Summer! summer! summer!'"

"The slackened wings dropped, the dying eyes looked landward, and then closed. But even as he fell, he believed himself sinking to rest on Mother Earth's kindly bosom, and he did not know it, when the cold waves buried him at sea."

"Oh, then, he *did* die!" cried the children, who, though they were tired of stories that end happily, yet, when they heard it, liked a sad ending no better than other children do (in which, by the bye, we hold them to be in the right, and can hardly forgive ourselves for chronicling this "ower true tale").

"Yes," said the old man, "he died; but it is said that the sweet dingle which was his home—forsaken by the nightingale—is regarded by birds as men regard a haunted house; for that at still summer midnight, when other thrushes sleep, a shadowy form, more like a skeleton leaf than a living bird, swings upon the tall tree-tops where he sat of old, and, rapt in a happy ecstasy, sings a song more sweet and joyous than thrush ever sang by day."

"Have you heard it?" asked the children.

The old man nodded. But not another word would he say. The children, however, forthwith began to lay plans for getting into the wood some mid-summer night, to test with their own ears the truth of his story, and to hear the spectre thrush's song. Whether the authorities permitted the expedition, and if not, whether the young people baffled their vigilance—whether they heard the song, and if so, whether they understood it—we are not empowered to tell here.

*   *   *   *   *

CHRISTMAS CRACKERS

A FANTASIA

It was Christmas-eve in an old-fashioned country-house, where Christmas was being kept with old-fashioned form and custom. It was getting late. The candles swaggered in their sockets, and the yule log glowed steadily like a red-hot coal.

"The fire has reached his heart," said the tutor: "he is warm all through. How red he is! He shines with heat and hospitality like some warm-hearted old gentleman when a convivial evening is pretty far advanced. To-morrow he will be as cold and grey as the morning after a festival, when the glasses are being washed up, and the host is calculating his expenses. Yes! you know it is so;" and the tutor nodded to the yule log as he spoke; and the log flared and crackled in return, till the tutor's face shone like his own. He had no other means of reply.

The tutor was grotesque-looking at any time. He was lank and meagre, with a long body and limbs, and high shoulders. His face was smooth-shaven, and his skin like old parchment stretched over high cheek-bones and lantern jaws; but in their hollow sockets his eyes gleamed with the changeful lustre of two precious gems. In the ruddy firelight they were

Juliana Horatia Ewing

like rubies, and when he drew back into the shade they glared green like the eyes of a cat. It must not be inferred from the tutor's presence this evening that there were no Christmas holidays in this house. They had begun some days before; and if the tutor had had a home to go to, it is to be presumed that he would have gone.

As the candles got lower, and the log flared less often, weird lights and shades, such as haunt the twilight, crept about the room. The tutor's shadow, longer, lanker, and more grotesque than himself, mopped and mowed upon the wall beside him. The snapdragon burnt blue, and as the raisin-hunters stirred the flaming spirit, the ghastly light made the tutor look so hideous that the widow's little boy was on the eve of howling, and spilled the raisins he had just secured. (He did not like putting his fingers into the flames, but he hovered near the more adventurous school-boys and collected the raisins that were scattered on the table by the hasty *grabs* of braver hands.)

The widow was a relative of the house. She had married a Mr. Jones, and having been during his life his devoted slave, had on his death transferred her allegiance to his son. The late Mr. Jones was a small man with a strong temper, a large appetite, and a taste for drawing-room theatricals. So Mrs. Jones had called her son Macready; "for," she said, "his poor papa would have made a fortune on the stage, and I wish to commemorate his talents. Besides, Macready sounds better with Jones than a commoner Christian name would do."

But his cousins called him MacGreedy.

"The apples of the enchanted garden were guarded by dragons. Many knights went after them. One wished for the apples, but he did not like to fight the dragons."

It was the tutor who spoke from the dark corner by the fire-place. His eyes shone like a cat's, and MacGreedy felt like a half-scared mouse, and made up his mind to cry. He put his right fist into one eye, and had just taken it out, and was about to put his left fist into the other, when he saw that the tutor was no longer looking at him. So he made up his mind to go on with the raisins, for one can have a peevish cry at any time, but plums are not scattered broadcast every day. Several times he had tried to pocket them, but just at the moment the tutor was sure to look at him, and in his fright he dropped the raisins, and never could find them again. So this time he resolved to eat them then and there. He had just put one into his mouth when the tutor leaned forward, and his eyes, glowing in the firelight, met MacGreedy's, who had not even the presence of mind to shut his mouth, but remained spellbound, with a raisin in his cheek.

Flicker, flack! The school-boys stirred up snapdragon again, and with the blue light upon his features the tutor made so horrible a grimace that MacGreedy swallowed the raisin with a start. He had bolted it whole, and it might have been a bread pill for any enjoyment he had of the flavour. But the tutor laughed aloud. He certainly was an alarming object, pulling those grimaces in the blue brandy glare; and unpleasantly like a picture of Bogy himself with horns and a tail, in a juvenile volume upstairs. True, there were no horns to speak of among the tutor's grizzled curls, and his coat seemed to fit as well as most people's on his long back, so that unless he put his tail in his pocket, it is difficult to see how he could have had one. But then (as Miss Letitia said) "With dress one can do anything and hide anything," and on dress Miss Letitia's opinion was final.

Miss Letitia was a cousin. She was dark, high-coloured, glossy-haired, stout, and showy. She was as neat as a new pin, and had a will of her own. Her hair was firmly fixed by

Juliana Horatia Ewing

bandoline, her garibaldis by an arrangement which failed when applied to those of the widow, and her opinions by the simple process of looking at everything from one point of view. Her *forte* was dress and general ornamentation; not that Miss Letitia was extravagant—far from it. If one may use the expression, she utilized for ornament a hundred bits and scraps that most people would have wasted. But, like other artists, she saw everything through the medium of her own art. She looked at birds with an eye to hats, and at flowers with reference to evening parties. At picture exhibitions and concerts she carried away jacket patterns and bonnets in her head, as other people make mental notes of an aerial effect, or a bit of fine instrumentation. An enthusiastic horticulturist once sent Miss Letitia a cut specimen of a new flower. It was a lovely spray from a lately-imported shrub. A botanist would have pressed it—an artist must have taken its portrait—a poet might have written a sonnet in praise of its beauty. Miss Letitia twisted a piece of wire round its stem, and fastened it on to her black lace bonnet. It came on the day of a review, when Miss Letitia had to appear in a carriage, and it was quite a success. As she said to the widow, "It was so natural that no one could doubt its being Parisian."

"What a strange fellow that tutor is!" said the visitor. He spoke to the daughter of the house, a girl with a face like a summer's day, and hair like a ripe corn-field rippling in the sun. He was a fine young man, and had a youth's taste for the sports and amusements of his age. But lately he had changed. He seemed to himself to be living in a higher, nobler atmosphere than hitherto. He had discovered that he was poetical —he might prove to be a genius. He certainly was eloquent, he could talk for hours, and did so—to the young lady with the sunshiny face. They spoke on the highest subjects, and what a listener she was! So intelligent and appreciative, and with such an exquisite *pose* of the head—it must inspire a block of wood merely to see such a creature in a listening attitude. As to our young friend, he poured forth volumes; he was really clever, and for her he became eloquent. To-night he spoke of Christmas, of time-honoured custom and old association; and what he said would have made a Christmas article for a magazine of the first class. He poured scorn on the cold nature that could not, and the affectation that would not, appreciate the domestic festivities of this sacred season. What, he asked, could be more delightful, more perfect than such a gathering as this, of the family circle round the Christmas hearth? He spoke with feeling, and it may be said with disinterested feeling, for he had not joined his family circle himself this Christmas, and there was a vacant place by the hearth of his own home.

"He is strange," said the young lady (she spoke of the tutor in answer to the above remark); "but I am very fond of him. He has been with us so long he is like one of the family; though we know as little of his history as we did on the day he came."

"He looks clever," said the visitor. (Perhaps that is the least one can say for a fellow-creature who shows a great deal of bare skull, and is not otherwise good-looking.)

"He is clever," she answered, "wonderfully clever; so clever and so odd that sometimes I fancy he is hardly 'canny.' There is something almost supernatural about his acuteness and his ingenuity, but they are so kindly used; I wonder he has not brought out any playthings for us to-night."

"Playthings?" inquired the young man.

"Yes; on birthdays or festivals like this he generally brings something out of those huge pockets of his. He has been all over the world, and he produces Indian puzzles, Japanese flower-buds that bloom in hot water, and German toys with complicated machinery, which I suspect him of manufacturing himself. I call him Godpapa Grosselmayer, after that delightful old fellow in Hoffman's tale of the Nut Cracker."

"What's that about crackers?" inquired the tutor, sharply, his eyes changing colour like a fire opal.

"I am talking of *Nussnacker und Mausekoenig,*" laughed the young lady. "Crackers do not belong to Christmas; fireworks come on the 5th of November."

"Tut, tut!" said the tutor; "I always tell your ladyship that you are still a tom-boy at heart, as when I first came, and you climbed trees and pelted myself and my young students with horse-chestnuts. You think of crackers to explode at the heels of timorous old gentlemen in a November fog; but I mean bonbon crackers, coloured crackers, dainty crackers— crackers for young people with mottoes of sentiment" (here the tutor shrugged his high shoulders an inch or two higher, and turned the palms of his hands outwards with a glance indescribably comical)—"crackers with paper prodigies, crackers with sweetmeats—*such* sweetmeats!" He smacked his lips with a grotesque contortion, and looked at Master McGreedy, who choked himself with his last raisin, and forthwith burst into tears.

The widow tried in vain to soothe him with caresses, but he only stamped and howled the more. But Miss Letitia gave him some smart smacks on the shoulders to cure his choking fit, and as she kept up the treatment with vigour, the young gentleman was obliged to stop and assure her that the raisin had "gone the right way" at last. "If he were my child," Miss Letitia had been known to observe, with that confidence which characterizes the theories of those who are not parents, "I would, &c., &c., &c.;" in fact, Miss Letitia thought she would have made a very different boy of him—as, indeed, I believe she would.

"Are crackers all that you have for us, sir?" asked one of the two school-boys, as they hung over the tutor's chair. They were twins, grand boys, with broad, good-humoured faces, and curly wigs, as like as two puppy dogs of the same breed. They were only known apart by their intimate friends, and were always together, romping, laughing, snarling, squabbling, huffing and helping each other against the world. Each of them owned a wiry terrier, and in their relations to each other the two dogs (who were marvellously alike) closely followed the example of their masters.

"Do you not care for crackers, Jim?" asked the tutor.

"Not much, sir. They do for girls: but, as you know, I care for nothing but military matters. Do you remember that beautiful toy of yours—'The Besieged City'? Ah! I liked that. Look out, Tom! you're shoving my arm. Can't you stand straight, man?'

"R-r-r-r—r-r, snap!"

Tom's dog was resenting contact with Jim's dog on the hearthrug. There was a hustle among the four, and then they subsided.

"The Besieged City was all very well for you, Jim," said Tom, who meant to be a sailor; "but please to remember that it admitted of no attack from the sea; and what was there for me to do? Ah, sir! you are so clever, I often think you could help me to make a swing with ladders instead of single ropes, so that I could run up and down the rigging whilst it was in full go."

"That would be something like your fir-tree prank, Tom," said his sister. "Can you believe," she added, turning to the visitor, "that Tom lopped the branches of a tall young fir-tree all the way up, leaving little bits for foothold, and then climbed up it one day in an awful storm of wind, and clung on at the top, rocking backwards and forwards? And when Papa sent word for him to come down, he said parental authority was superseded at sea by the rules of the service. It was a dreadful storm, and the tree snapped very soon after he got safe to the ground."

"Storm!" sneered Tom, "a capful of wind. Well, it did blow half a gale at the last. But oh! it was glorious!"

"Let us see what we can make of the crackers," said the tutor—and he pulled some out of his pocket. They were put in a dish upon the table, for the company to choose from; and the terriers jumped and snapped, and tumbled over each other, for they thought that the plate contained eatables. Animated by the same idea, but with quieter steps, Master MacGreedy also approached the table.

"The dogs are noisy," said the tutor, "too noisy. We must have quiet—peace and quiet." His lean hand was once more in his pocket, and he pulled out a box, from which he took some powder, which he scattered on the burning log. A slight smoke now rose from the hot embers, and floated into the room. Was the powder one of those strange compounds that act upon the brain? Was it a magician's powder? Who knows? With it came a sweet, subtle fragrance. It was strange—every one fancied he had smelt it before, and all were absorbed in wondering what it was, and where they had met with it. Even the dogs sat on their haunches with their noses up, sniffing in a speculative manner.

"It's not lavender," said the grandmother, slowly, "and it's not rosemary. There is a something of tansy in it (and a very fine tonic flavour too, my dears, though it's *not* in fashion now). Depend upon it, it's a potpourri, and from an excellent receipt, sir"—and the old lady bowed courteously towards the tutor. "My mother made the best potpourri in the county, and it was very much like this. Not quite, perhaps, but much the same, much the same."

The grandmother was a fine old gentlewoman "of the old school," as the phrase is. She was very stately and gracious in her manners, daintily neat in her person, and much attached to the old parson of the parish, who now sat near her chair. All her life she had been very proud of her fine stock of fair linen, both household and personal; and for many years past had kept her own graveclothes ready in a drawer. They were bleached as white as snow, and lay amongst bags of dried lavender and potpourri. Many times had it seemed likely that they would be needed, for the old lady had had severe illnesses of late, when the good parson sat by her bedside, and read to her of the coming of the Bridegroom, and of that "fine linen clean and white," which is "the righteousness of the saints." It was of that drawer, with its lavender and potpourri bags, that the scented smoke had reminded her.

"It has rather an overpowering odour," said the old parson; "it is suggestive of incense. I am sure I once smelt something like it in the Church of the Nativity at Bethlehem. It is very delicious."

The parson's long residence in his parish had been marked by one great holiday. With the savings of many years he had performed a pilgrimage to the Holy Land; and it was rather a joke against him that he illustrated a large variety of subjects by reference to his favourite topic, the holiday of his life.

"It smells of gunpowder," said Jim, decidedly, "and something else. I can't tell what."

"Something one smells in a seaport town," said Tom.

"Can't be very delicious then," Jim retorted.

"It's not *quite* the same," piped the widow; "but it reminds me very much of an old bottle of attar of roses that was given to me when I was at school, with a copy of verses, by a young gentleman who was brother to one of the pupils. I remember Mr. Jones was quite annoyed when he found it in an old box, where I am sure I had not touched it for ten years or more; and I never spoke to him but once, on Examination Day (the young gentleman, I mean). And its like—yes it's certainly like a hair-wash Mr. Jones used to use. I've forgotten what it was called, but I know it cost fifteen shillings a bottle; and Macready threw one over a few weeks before his dear papa's death, and annoyed him extremely."

Whilst the company were thus engaged, Master MacGreedy took advantage of the general abstraction to secure half-a-dozen crackers to his own share; he retired to a corner with them, where he meant to pick them quietly to pieces by himself. He wanted the gay paper, and the motto, and the sweetmeats; but he did not like the report of the cracker. And then what he did want, he wanted all to himself.

"Give us a cracker," said Master Jim, dreamily.

The dogs, after a few dissatisfied snorts, had dropped from their sitting posture, and were lying close together on the rug, dreaming and uttering short commenting barks and whines at intervals. The twins were now reposing lazily at the tutor's feet, and did not feel disposed to exert themselves even so far as to fetch their own bonbons.

"There's one," said the tutor, taking a fresh cracker from his pocket. One end of it was of red and gold paper, the other of transparent green stuff with silver lines. The boys pulled it.

* * * * *

The report was louder than Jim had expected. "The firing has begun," he murmured, involuntarily; "steady, steady!" these last words were to his horse, who seemed to be moving under him, not from fear, but from impatience. What had been the red and gold paper of the cracker was now the scarlet and gold lace of his own cavalry uniform. He knocked a speck from his sleeve, and scanned the distant ridge, from which a thin line of smoke floated solemnly away, with keen, impatient eyes. Were they to stand inactive all the day?

Presently the horse erects his head. His eyes sparkle—he pricks his sensitive ears—his nostrils quiver with a strange delight. It is the trumpet! Fan farra! Fan farra! The brazen voice speaks—the horses move—the plumes wave—the helmets shine. On a summer's day they ride slowly, gracefully, calmly down a slope, to Death or Glory. Fan farra! Fan farra! Fan farra!

* * * * *

Of all this Master Tom knew nothing. The report of the cracker seemed to him only an echo in his brain of a sound that had been in his ears for thirty-six weary hours. The noise of a heavy sea beating against the ship's side in a gale. It was over now, and he was keeping the midnight watch on deck, gazing upon the liquid green of the waves, which, heaving and seething after storm, were lit with phosphoric light, and as the ship held steadily on her course, poured past at the rate of twelve knots an hour in a silvery stream. Faster than any ship can sail his thoughts travelled home; and as old times came back to him, he hardly knew whether what he looked at was the phosphor-lighted sea, or green gelatine paper barred with silver. And did the tutor speak? Or was it the voice of some sea-monster sounding in his ears?

"The spirits of the storm have gone below to make their report. The treasure gained from sunk vessels has been reckoned, and the sea is illuminated in honour of the spoil."

*　*　*　*　*

The visitor now took a cracker and held it to the young lady. Her end was of white paper with a raised pattern; his of dark-blue gelatine with gold stars. It snapped, the bonbon dropped between them, and the young man got the motto. It was a very bald one—

"My heart is thine.
Wilt thou be mine?"

He was ashamed to show it to her. What could be more meagre? One could write a hundred better couplets "standing on one leg," as the saying is. He was trying to improvise just one for the occasion, when he became aware that the blue sky over his head was dark with the shades of night, and lighted with stars. A brook rippled near with a soothing monotony. The evening wind sighed through the trees, and wafted the fragrance of the sweet bay-leaved willow towards him, and blew a stray lock of hair against his face. Yes! *She* also was there, walking beside him, under the scented willow-bushes. Where, why, and whither he did not ask to know. She was with him—with him; and he seemed to tread on the summer air. He had no doubt as to the nature of his own feelings for her, and here was such an opportunity for declaring them as might never occur again. Surely now, if ever, he would be eloquent! Thoughts of poetry clothed in words of fire must spring unbidden to his lips at such a moment. And yet somehow he could not find a single word to say. He beat his brains, but not an idea would come forth. Only that idiotic cracker motto, which haunted him with its meagre couplet:

"My heart is thine.
Wilt thou be mine?"

Meanwhile they wandered on. The precious time was passing. He must at least make a beginning.

"What a fine night it is!" he observed. But, oh dear! that was a thousand times balder and more meagre than the cracker motto; and not another word could he find to say. At this moment the awkward silence was broken by a voice from a neighbouring copse. It was a nightingale singing to his mate. There was no lack of eloquence, and of melodious eloquence, there. The song was as plaintive as old memories, and as full of tenderness as the eyes of the young girl were full of tears. They were standing still now, and with her graceful head bent she was listening to the bird. He stooped his head near hers, and spoke with a simple natural outburst almost involuntary.

"Do you ever think of old times? Do you remember the old house, and the fun we used to have? and the tutor whom you pelted with horse-chestnuts when you were a little girl? And those cracker bonbons, and the motto *we* drew—

'My heart is thine.
Wilt thou be mine?'"

She smiled, and lifted her eyes ("blue as the sky, and bright as the stars," he thought) to his, and answered "Yes."

Juliana Horatia Ewing

Then the bonbon motto was avenged, and there was silence. Eloquent, perfect, complete, beautiful silence! Only the wind sighed through the fragrant willows, the stream rippled, the stars shone, and in the neighbouring copse the nightingale sang, and sang, and sang.

* * * * *

When the white end of the cracker came into the young lady's hand, she was full of admiration for the fine raised pattern. As she held it between her fingers it suddenly struck her that she had discovered what the tutor's fragrant smoke smelt like. It was like the scent of orange-flowers, and had certainly a soporific effect upon the senses. She felt very sleepy, and as she stroked the shiny surface of the cracker she found herself thinking it was very soft for paper, and then rousing herself with a start, and wondering at her own folly in speaking thus of the white silk in which she was dressed, and of which she was holding up the skirt between her finger and thumb, as if she were dancing a minuet.

"It's grandmamma's egg-shell brocade!" she cried. "Oh, Grandmamma! Have you given it to me? That lovely old thing! But I thought it was the family wedding-dress, and that I was not to have it till I was a bride."

"And so you are, my dear. And a fairer bride the sun never shone on," sobbed the old lady, who was kissing and blessing her, and wishing her, in the words of the old formula—

"Health to wear it,
Strength to tear it,
And money to buy another."

"There is no hope for the last two things, you know," said the young girl; "for I am sure that the flag that braved a thousand years was not half so strong as your brocade; and as to buying another, there are none to be bought in these degenerate days."

The old lady's reply was probably very gracious, for she liked to be complimented on the virtues of old things in general, and of her egg-shell brocade in particular. But of what she said her granddaughter heard nothing. With the strange irregularity of dreams, she found herself, she knew not how, in the old church. It was true. She was a bride, standing there with old friends and old associations thick around her, on the threshold of a new life. The sun shone through the stained glass of the windows, and illuminated the brocade, whose old-fashioned stiffness so became her childish beauty, and flung a thousand new tints over her sunny hair, and drew so powerful a fragrance from the orange-blossom with which it was twined, that it was almost overpowering. Yes! It was too sweet—too strong. She certainly would not be able to bear it much longer without losing her senses. And the service was going on. A question had been asked of her, and she must reply. She made a strong effort, and said "Yes," simply and very earnestly, for it was what she meant. But she had no sooner said it than she became uneasily conscious that she had not used the right words. Some one laughed. It was the tutor, and his voice jarred and disturbed the dream, as a stone troubles the surface of still water. The vision trembled, and then broke, and the young lady found herself still sitting by the table and fingering the cracker paper, whilst the tutor chuckled and rubbed his hands by the fire, and his shadow scrambled on the wall like an ape upon a tree. But her "Yes" had passed into the young man's dream without disturbing it, and he dreamt on.

It was a cracker like the preceding one that the grandmother and the parson pulled together. The old lady had insisted

Juliana Horatia Ewing

upon it. The good rector had shown a tendency to low spirits this evening, and a wish to withdraw early. But the old lady did not approve of people "shirking" (as boys say) either their duties or their pleasures; and to keep a "merry Christmas" in a family circle that had been spared to meet in health and happiness, seemed to her to be both the one and the other.

It was his sermon for next day which weighed on the parson's mind. Not that he was behindhand with that part of his duties. He was far too methodical in his habits for that, and it had been written before the bustle of Christmas week began. But after preaching Christmas sermons from the same pulpit for thirty-five years, he felt keenly how difficult it is to awaken due interest in subjects that are so familiar, and to give new force to lessons so often repeated. So he wanted a quiet hour in his own study before he went to rest, with the sermon that did not satisfy him, and the subject that should be so heart-stirring and ever-new,—the Story of Bethlehem.

He consented, however, to pull one cracker with the grand-mother, though he feared the noise might startle her nerves, and said so.

"Nerves were not invented in my young days," said the old lady, firmly; and she took her part in the ensuing explosion without so much as a wink.

As the cracker snapped, it seemed to the parson as if the fragrant smoke from the yule log were growing denser in the room. Through the mist from time to time the face of the tutor loomed large, and then disappeared. At last the clouds rolled away, and the parson breathed clear air. Clear, yes, and how clear! This brilliant freshness, these intense lights and shadows, this mildness and purity in the night air—

"It is not England," he muttered, "it is the East. I have felt no air like this since I breathed the air of Palestine."

Over his head, through immeasurable distances, the dark blue space was lighted by the great multitude of the stars, whose glittering ranks have in that atmosphere a distinctness and a glory unseen with us. Perhaps no scene of beauty in the visible creation has proved a more hackneyed theme for the poet and the philosopher than a starry night. But not all the superabundance of simile and moral illustration with which the subject has been loaded can rob the beholder of the freshness of its grandeur or the force of its teaching; that noblest and most majestic vision of the handiwork of GOD on which the eye of man is here permitted to rest.

As the parson gazed he became conscious that he was not alone. Other eyes besides his were watching the skies to-night. Dark, profound, patient, Eastern eyes, used from the cradle to the grave to watch and wait. The eyes of star-gazers and dream-interpreters; men who believed the fate of empires to be written in shining characters on the face of heaven, as the "Mene, Mene," was written in fire on the walls of the Babylonian palace. The old parson was one of the many men of real learning and wide reading who pursue their studies in the quiet country parishes of England, and it was with the keen interest of intelligence that he watched the group of figures that lay near him.

"Is this a vision of the past?" he asked himself. "There can be no doubt as to these men. They are star-gazers, magi, and, from their dress and bearing, men of high rank; perhaps 'teachers of a higher wisdom' in one of the purest philoso-phies of the old heathen world. When one thinks," he pursued, "of the intense interest, the eager excitement which the student of history finds in the narrative of the past as unfolded in dusty records written by the hand of man, one

Juliana Horatia Ewing

may realize how absorbing must have been that science which professed to unveil the future, and to display to the eyes of the wise the fate of dynasties written with the finger of GOD amid the stars."

The dark-robed figures were so still that they might almost have been carved in stone. The air seemed to grow purer and purer; the stars shone brighter and brighter; suspended in ether the planets seemed to hang like lamps. Now a shooting meteor passed athwart the sky, and vanished behind the hill. But not for this did the watchers move; in silence they watched on—till, on a sudden, how and whence the parson knew not, across the shining ranks of that immeasurable host, whose names and number are known to GOD alone, there passed in slow but obvious motion one brilliant solitary star—a star of such surpassing brightness that he involuntarily joined in the wild cry of joy and greeting with which the Men of the East now prostrated themselves with their faces to the earth. He could not understand the language in which, with noisy clamour and gesticulation, they broke their former profound and patient silence, and greeted the portent for which they had watched. But he knew now that these were the Wise Men of the Epiphany, and that this was the Star of Bethlehem. In his ears rang the energetic simplicity of the Gospel narrative, "When they saw the Star, they rejoiced with exceeding great joy."

With exceeding great joy! Ah! happy magi, who (more blest than Balaam the son of Beor) were faithful to the dim light vouchsafed to you; the Gentile Church may well be proud of your memory. Ye travelled long and far to bring royal offerings to the King of the Jews, with a faith not found in Israel. Ye saw Him whom prophets and kings had desired to see, and were glad. Wise men indeed, and wise with the highest wisdom, in that ye suffered yourselves to be taught of GOD.

Then the parson prayed that if this were indeed a dream he might dream on; might pass, if only in a vision, over the hill, following the footsteps of the magi, whilst the Star went before them, till he should see it rest above that city, which, little indeed among the thousands of Judah, was yet the birthplace of the Lord's Christ.

"Ah!" he almost sobbed, "let me follow! On my knees let me follow into the house and see the Holy Child. In the eyes of how many babies I have seen mind and thought far beyond their powers of communication, every mother knows. But if at times, with a sort of awe, one sees the immortal soul shining through the prison-bars of helpless infancy, what, oh! what must it be to behold the GOD-head veiled in flesh through the face of a little child!"

The parson stretched out his arms, but even with the passion of his words the vision began to break. He dared not move for fear it should utterly fade, and as he lay still and silent, the wise men roused their followers, and, led by the Star, the train passed solemnly over the distant hills.

Then the clear night became clouded with fragrant vapour, and with a sigh the parson awoke.

* * * * *

When the cracker snapped and the white end was left in the grandmother's hand, she was astonished to perceive (as she thought) that the white lace veil which she had worn over her wedding bonnet was still in her possession, and that she was turning it over in her fingers. "I fancied I gave it to Jemima when her first baby was born," she muttered dreamily. It was darned and yellow, but it carried her back all the same, and recalled happy hours with wonderful vividness. She remembered the post-chaise and the postillion. "He was such a pert little fellow, and how we laughed at him! He must be either dead or a very shaky old man by now," said the old lady. She seemed to smell the scent of meadow-sweet that was so powerful in a lane through which they drove; and how clearly she could see the clean little country inn where they spent the honeymoon! She seemed to be there now, taking off her bonnet and shawl, in the quaint clean chamber, with the heavy oak rafters, and the jasmine coming in at the window, and glancing with pardonable pride at the fair face reflected in the mirror. But as she laid her things on the patchwork coverlet, it seemed to her that the lace veil became fine white linen, and was folded about a figure that lay in the bed; and when she looked round the room again everything was draped in white—white blinds hung before the windows, and even the old oak chest and the press were covered with clean white cloths, after the decent custom of the country; whilst from the church tower without the passing bell tolled slowly. She had not seen the face of the corpse, and a strange anxiety came over her to count the strokes of the bell, which tell if it is a man, woman, or child who has passed away. One, two, three, four, five, six, seven! No more. It was a woman, and when she looked on the face of the dead she saw her own. But even as she looked the fair linen of the grave-clothes became the buoyant drapery of another figure, in whose face she found a strange recognition of the lineaments of the dead with all the loveliness of the bride. But ah! more, much more! On that face there was a beauty not doomed to wither, before those happy eyes lay a future unshadowed by the imperfections of earthly prospects, and the folds of that robe were white as no fuller on earth can white them. The window curtain parted, the jasmine flowers bowed their heads, the spirit passed from the chamber of death, and the old lady's dream was ended.

* * * * *

Miss Letitia had shared a cracker with the widow. The widow squeaked when the cracker went off, and then insisted upon giving up the smart paper and everything to Miss Letitia. She had always given up everything to Mr. Jones, she did so now to Master MacGreedy, and was quite unaccustomed to keep anything for her own share. She did not give this explanation herself, but so it was.

The cracker that thus fell into the hands of Miss Letitia was one of those new-fashioned ones that have a paper pattern of some article of dress wrapped up in them instead of a bonbon. This one was a paper bonnet made in the latest *mode*—of green tissue-paper; and Miss Letitia stuck it on the top of her chignon, with an air that the widow envied from the bottom of her heart. She had not the gift of "carrying off" her clothes. But to the tutor, on the contrary, it seemed to afford the most extreme amusement; and as Miss Letitia bowed gracefully hither and thither in the energy of her conversation with the widow, the green paper fluttering with each emphasis, he fairly shook with delight, his shadow dancing like a maniac beside him. He had scattered some more powder on the coals, and it may have been that the smoke got into her eyes, and confused her ideas of colour, but Miss Letitia was struck with a fervid and otherwise unaccountable admiration for the paper ends of the cracker, which were most unusually ugly. One was of a sallowish salmon-colour, and transparent, the other was of brick-red paper with a fringe. As Miss Letitia turned them over, she saw, to her unspeakable delight, that there were several yards of each material, and her peculiar genius instantly seized upon the fact that in the present rage for double skirts there might be enough of the two kinds to combine into a fashionable dress.

It had never struck her before that a dirty salmon went well with brick-red. "They blend so becomingly, my dear," she

Juliana Horatia Ewing

murmured; "and I think the under-skirt will sit well, it is so stiff."

The widow did not reply. The fumes of the tutor's compound made her sleepy, and though she nodded to Miss Letitia's observations, it was less from appreciation of their force, than from inability to hold up her head. She was dreaming uneasy, horrible dreams, like nightmares; in which from time to time there mingled expressions of doubt and dissatisfaction which fell from Miss Letitia's lips. "Just half-a-yard short—no gores—false hem," (and the melancholy reflection that) "flounces take so much stuff." Then the tutor's face kept appearing and vanishing with horrible grimaces through the mist. At last the widow fell fairly asleep, and dreamed that she was married to the Blue Beard of nursery annals, and that on his return from his memorable journey he had caught her in the act of displaying the mysterious cupboard to Miss Letitia. As he waved his scimitar over her head, he seemed unaccountably to assume the form and features of the tutor. In her agitation the poor woman could think of no plea against his severity, except that the cupboard was already crammed with the corpses of his previous wives, and there was no room for her. She was pleading this argument when Miss Letitia's voice broke in upon her dream with decisive accent:

"There's enough for two bodies."

The widow shrieked and awoke.

"High and low," explained Miss Letitia. "My dear, what *are* you screaming about?"

"I am very sorry indeed," said the widow; "I beg your pardon, I'm sure, a thousand times. But since Mr. Jones's death I have been so nervous, and I had such a horrible dream. And, oh dear! oh dear!" she added, "what is the matter with my precious child? Macready, love, come to your mamma, my pretty lamb."

Ugh! ugh! There were groans from the corner where Master MacGreedy sat on his crackers as if they were eggs, and he hatching them. He had only touched one, as yet, of the stock he had secured. He had picked it to pieces, had avoided the snap, and had found a large comfit like an egg with a rough shell inside. Every one knows that the goodies in crackers are not of a very superior quality. There is a large amount of white lead in the outside thinly disguised by a shabby flavour of sugar. But that outside once disposed of, there lies an almond at the core. Now an almond is a very delicious thing in itself, and doubly nice when it takes the taste of white paint and chalk out of one's mouth. But in spite of all the white lead and sugar and chalk through which he had sucked his way, MacGreedy could not come to the almond. A dozen times had he been on the point of spitting out the delusive sweetmeat; but just as he thought of it he was sure to feel a bit of hard rough edge, and thinking he had gained the kernel at last, he held valiantly on. It only proved to be a rough bit of sugar, however, and still the interminable coating melted copiously in his mouth; and still the clean, fragrant almond evaded his hopes. At last with a groan he spat the seemingly undiminished bonbon on to the floor, and turned as white and trembling as an arrowroot blanc-mange.

In obedience to the widow's entreaties the tutor opened a window, and tried to carry MacGreedy to the air; but that young gentleman utterly refused to allow the tutor to approach him, and was borne howling to bed by his mamma.

With the fresh air the fumes of the fragrant smoke dispersed, and the company roused themselves.

Juliana Horatia Ewing

"Rather oppressive, eh?" said the master of the house, who had had his dream too, with which we have no concern.

The dogs had had theirs also, and had testified to the same in their sleep by low growls and whines. Now they shook themselves, and rubbed against each other, growling in a warlike manner through their teeth, and wagging peaceably with their little stumpy tails.

The twins shook themselves, and fell to squabbling as to whether they had been to sleep or no; and, if either, which of them had given way to that weakness.

Miss Letitia took the paper bonnet from her head with a nervous laugh, and after looking regretfully at the cracker papers put them in her pocket.

The parson went home through the frosty night. In the village street he heard a boy's voice singing two lines of the Christian hymn—

"Trace we the Babe Who hath redeemed our loss
From the poor Manger to the bitter Cross;"

and his eyes filled with tears.

The old lady went to bed and slept in peace.

"In all the thirty-five years we have been privileged to hear you, sir," she told the rector next day after service, "I never heard such a Christmas sermon before."

The visitor carefully preserved the blue paper and the cracker motto. He came down early next morning to find the white half to put with them. He did not find it, for the young lady had taken it the night before.

The tutor had been in the room before him, wandering round the scene of the evening's festivities.

The yule log lay black and cold upon the hearth, and the tutor nodded to it. "I told you how it would be," he said; "but never mind, you have had your day, and a merry one too." In the corner lay the heap of crackers which Master MacGreedy had been too ill to remember when he retired. The tutor pocketed them with a grim smile.

As to the comfit, it was eaten by one of the dogs, who had come down earliest of all. He swallowed it whole, so whether it contained an almond or not, remains a mystery to the present time.

*   *   *   *   *

AMELIA AND THE DWARFS

My godmother's grandmother knew a good deal about the fairies. *Her* grandmother had seen a fairy rade on a Roodmas Eve, and she herself could remember a copper vessel of a queer shape which had been left by the elves on some occasion at an old farm-house among the hills, The following story came from her, and where she got it I do not know. She used to say it was a pleasant tale, with a good moral in the inside of it. My godmother often observed that a tale without a moral was like a nut without a kernel; not worth the cracking. (We called fire-side stories "cracks" in our part of the country.) This is the tale.

AMELIA

A couple of gentlefolk once lived in a certain part of England. (My godmother never would tell the name either of the place or the people, even if she knew it. She said one ought not to expose one's neighbours' failings more than there was due occasion for.) They had an only child, a daughter, whose name was Amelia. They were an easy-going, good-humoured couple; "rather soft," my godmother said, but she was apt to think anybody "soft" who came from the southern shires, as these people did. Amelia, who had been born farther north, was by no means so. She had a strong resolute will, and a clever head of her own, though she was but a child. She had a way of her own too, and had it very completely. Perhaps because she was an only child, or perhaps because they were so easy-going, her parents spoiled her. She was, beyond question, the most tiresome little girl in that or any other neighbourhood. From her baby days her father and mother had taken every opportunity of showing her to their friends, and there was not a friend who did not dread the infliction. When the good lady visited her acquaintances, she always took Amelia with her, and if the acquaintances were fortunate enough to see from the windows who was coming, they used to snatch up any delicate knick-knacks, or brittle ornaments lying about, and put them away, crying, "What is to be done? Here comes Amelia!"

When Amelia came in, she would stand and survey the room, whilst her mother saluted her acquaintance; and if anything struck her fancy, she would interrupt the greetings to draw her mother's attention to it, with a twitch of her shawl, "Oh, look, Mamma, at that funny bird in the glass case!" or perhaps, "Mamma, Mamma! There's a new carpet since we were here last;" for, as her mother said, she was "a very observing child."

Then she would wander round the room, examining and fingering everything, and occasionally coming back with something in her hand to tread on her mother's dress, and break in upon the ladies' conversation with—"Mamma! Mamma! What's the good of keeping this old basin? It's been broken and mended, and some of the pieces are quite loose now. I can feel them:" or—addressing the lady of the house —"That's not a real ottoman in the corner. It's a box covered with chintz. I know, for I've looked."

Then her mamma would say, reprovingly, "My *dear* Amelia!"

Juliana Horatia Ewing

And perhaps the lady of the house would beg, "Don't play with that old china, my love; for though it is mended, it is very valuable;" and her mother would add, "My dear Amelia, you must not."

Sometimes the good lady said, "You *must* not." Sometimes she tried—"You must *not*" When both these failed, and Amelia was balancing the china bowl on her finger-ends, her mamma would get flurried, and when Amelia flurried her, she always rolled her r's, and emphasized her words, so that it sounded thus:

"My dear-r-r-r-Ramelia! You must not."

At which Amelia would not so much as look round, till perhaps the bowl slipped from her fingers, and was smashed into unmendable fragments. Then her mamma would exclaim, "Oh, dear-r-r-r, oh, dear-r-Ramelia" and the lady of the house would try to look as if it did not matter, and when Amelia and her mother departed, would pick up the bits, and pour out her complaints to her lady friends, most of whom had suffered many such damages at the hands of this "very observing child."

When the good couple received their friends at home, there was no escaping from Amelia. If it was a dinner-party, she came in with the dessert, or perhaps sooner. She would take up her position near some one, generally the person most deeply engaged in conversation, and either lean heavily against him or her, or climb on to his or her knee, without being invited. She would break in upon the most interesting discussion with her own little childish affairs, in the following style—"I've been out to-day. I walked to the town. I jumped across three brooks. Can you jump? Papa gave me sixpence to-day. I am saving up my money to be rich. You may cut me an orange; no, I'll take it to Mr. Brown, he peels it with a spoon and turns the skin back. Mr. Brown! Mr. Brown! Don't talk to Mamma, but peel me an orange, please. Mr. Brown! I'm playing with your finger-glass."

And when the finger-glass full of cold water had been upset on to Mr. Brown's shirt-front, Amelia's mamma would cry— "Oh dear, oh dear-r-Ramelia!" and carry her off with the ladies to the drawing-room.

Here she would scramble on to the ladies' knees, or trample out the gathers of their dresses, and fidget with their orna- ments, startling some luckless lady by the announcement, "I've got your bracelet undone at last!" who would find one of the divisions broken open by force, Amelia not understanding the working of a clasp.

Or perhaps two young lady friends would get into a quiet corner for a chat. The observing child would sure to spy them, and run on to them, crushing their flowers and ribbons, and crying—"You two want to talk secrets, I know. I can hear what you say. I'm going to listen, I am. And I shall tell, too;" when perhaps a knock at the door announced the Nurse to take Miss Amelia to bed, and spread a general rapture of relief.

Then Amelia would run to trample and worry her mother, and after much teasing, and clinging, and complaining, the Nurse would be dismissed, and the fond mamma would turn to the lady next to her, and say with a smile—"I suppose I must let her stay up a little. It is such a treat to her, poor child!"

But it was no treat to the visitors.

Besides tormenting her fellow-creatures, Amelia had a trick of teasing animals. She was really fond of dogs, but she was still fonder of doing what she was wanted not to do, and of worrying everything and everybody about her. So she used to tread on the tips of their tails, and pretend to give them biscuit, and then hit them on the nose, besides pulling at those few, long, sensitive hairs which thin-skinned dogs wear on the upper lip.

Now Amelia's mother's acquaintances were so very well-bred and amiable, that they never spoke their minds to either the mother or the daughter about what they endured from the latter's rudeness, wilfulness, and powers of destruction. But this was not the case with the dogs, and they expressed their sentiments by many a growl and snap. At last one day Amelia was tormenting a snow-white bulldog (who was certainly as well-bred and as amiable as any living creature in the kingdom), and she did not see that even his patience was becoming worn out. His pink nose became crimson with increased irritation, his upper lip twitched over his teeth, behind which he was rolling as many warning R's as Amelia's mother herself. She finally held out a bun towards him, and just as he was about to take it, she snatched it away and kicked him instead. This fairly exasperated the bulldog, and as Amelia would not let him bite the bun, he bit Amelia's leg.

Her mamma was so distressed that she fell into hysterics, and hardly knew what she was saying. She said the bulldog must be shot for fear he should go mad, and Amelia's wound must be done with a red-hot poker for fear *she* should go mad (with hydrophobia). And as of course she couldn't bear the pain of this, she must have chloroform, and she would most probably die of that; for as one in several thousands dies annually under chloroform, it was evident that her chance of life was very small indeed. So, as the poor lady said, "Whether we shoot Amelia and burn the bulldog—at least I mean shoot the bulldog and burn Amelia with a red-hot poker—or leave it alone; and whether Amelia or the bulldog has chloroform or bears it without—it seems to be death or madness every way!"

And as the doctor did not come fast enough, she ran out without her bonnet to meet him, and Amelia's papa, who was very much distressed too, ran after her with her bonnet. Meanwhile the doctor came in by another way, and found Amelia sitting on the dining-room floor with the bulldog, and crying bitterly. She was telling him that they wanted to shoot him, but that they should not, for it was all her fault and not his. But she did not tell him that she was to be burnt with a red-hot poker, for she thought it might hurt his feelings. And then she wept afresh, and kissed the bulldog, and the bulldog kissed her with his red tongue, and rubbed his pink nose against her, and beat his own tail much harder on the floor than Amelia had ever hit it. She said the same things to the doctor, but she told him also that she was willing to be burnt without chloroform if it must be done, and if they would spare the bulldog. And though she looked very white, she meant what she said.

But the doctor looked at her leg, and found that it was only a snap, and not a deep wound; and then he looked at the bulldog, and saw that so far from looking mad, he looked a great deal more sensible than anybody in the house. So he only washed Amelia's leg and bound it up, and she was not burnt with the poker, neither did she get hydrophobia; but she had got a good lesson on manners, and thenceforward she always behaved with the utmost propriety to animals, though she tormented her mother's friends as much as ever.

Now although Amelia's mamma's acquaintances were too polite to complain before her face, they made up for it by what they said behind her back. In allusion to the poor lady's ineffectual remonstrances, one gentleman said that the more mischief Amelia did, the dearer she seemed to grow to her mother. And somebody else replied that however dear she might be as a daughter, she was certainly a very *dear* friend, and proposed that they should send in a bill for all the damages she had done in the course of the year, as a round robin to her parents at Christmas. From which it may be seen that Amelia was not popular with her parents' friends, as (to do grown-up people justice) good children almost invariably are.

If she was not a favourite in the drawing-room, she was still less so in the nursery, where, besides all the hardships naturally belonging to attendance on a spoilt child, the poor Nurse was kept, as she said, "on the continual go" by Amelia's reckless destruction of her clothes. It was not fair wear and tear, it was not an occasional fall in the mire, or an accidental rent or two during a game at "Hunt the Hare," but it was constant wilful destruction, which Nurse had to repair as best she might. No entreaties would induce Amelia to "take care" of anything. She walked obstinately on the muddy side of the road when Nurse pointed out the clean parts, kicking up the dirt with her feet; if she climbed a wall she never tried to free her dress if it had caught; on she rushed, and half a skirt might be left behind for any care she had in the matter. "They must be mended," or "They must be washed," was all she thought about it.

"You seem to think things clean and mend themselves, Miss Amelia," said poor Nurse one day.

"No, I don't," said Amelia, rudely. "I think you do them; what are you here for?"

But though she spoke in this insolent and unlady-like fashion, Amelia really did not realize what the tasks were which her carelessness imposed on other people. When every hour of Nurse's day had been spent in struggling to keep her wilful young lady regularly fed, decently dressed, and moderately well behaved (except, indeed, those hours when her mother was fighting the same battle down-stairs); and when at last, after the hardest struggle of all, she had been got to bed not more than two hours later than her appointed time, even then there was no rest for Nurse. Amelia's mamma could at last lean back in her chair and have a quiet chat with her husband, which was not broken in upon every two minutes, and Amelia herself was asleep; but Nurse must sit up for hours wearing out her eyes by the light of a tallow candle, in fine-darning great, jagged, and most unnecessary holes in Amelia's muslin dresses. Or perhaps she had to wash and iron clothes for Amelia's wear next day. For sometimes she was so very destructive, that towards the end of the week she had used up all her clothes and had no clean ones to fall back upon.

Amelia's meals were another source of trouble. She would not wear a pinafore; if it had been put on, she would burst the strings, and perhaps in throwing it away knock her plate of mutton broth over the tablecloth and her own dress. Then she fancied first one thing and then another; she did not like this or that; she wanted a bit cut here or there. Her mamma used to begin by saying, "My dear-r-Ramelia, you must not be so wasteful," and she used to end by saying, "The dear child has positively no appetite;" which seemed to be a good reason for not wasting any more food upon her; but with Amelia's mamma it only meant that she might try a little cutlet and tomato sauce when she had half finished her roast beef, and that most of the cutlet and all the mashed potato might be exchanged for plum tart and custard; and that when she had spooned up the custard and played with the paste, and put the plum stones on the tablecloth, she might be tempted with a little Stilton cheese and celery, and exchange that for anything that caught her fancy in the dessert dishes.

The Nurse used to say, "Many a poor child would thank GOD for what you waste every meal-time, Miss Amelia," and to quote a certain good old saying, "Waste not, want not." But Amelia's mamma allowed her to send away on her plates what would have fed another child, day after day.

UNDER THE HAYCOCKS

It was summer, and haytime. Amelia had been constantly in the hayfield, and the haymakers had constantly wished that she had been anywhere else. She mislaid the rakes, nearly killed herself and several other persons with a fork, and overturned one haycock after another as fast as they were made. At tea-time it was hoped that she would depart, but she teased her mamma to have the tea brought into the field, and her mamma said, "The poor child must have a treat sometimes," and so it was brought out.

After this she fell off the haycart, and was a good deal shaken, but not hurt. So she was taken indoors, and the haymakers worked hard and cleared the field, all but a few cocks which were left till the morning.

The sun set, the dew fell, the moon rose. It was a lovely night. Amelia peeped from behind the blinds of the drawing-room windows, and saw four haycocks, each with a deep shadow reposing at its side. The rest of the field was swept clean, and looked pale in the moonshine. It was a lovely night.

"I want to go out," said Amelia. "They will take away those cocks before I can get at them in the morning, and there will be no more jumping and tumbling, I shall go out and have some fun now."

"My dear Amelia, you must not," said her mamma; and her papa added, "I won't hear of it." So Amelia went up-stairs to grumble to Nurse; but Nurse only said, "Now, my dear Miss Amelia, do go quietly to bed, like a dear love. The field is all wet with dew. Besides, it's a moonlight night, and who knows what's abroad? You might see the fairies—bless us and sain us!—and what not. There's been a magpie hopping up and down near the house all day, and that's a sign of ill-luck."

"I don't care for magpies," said Amelia; "I threw a stone at that one to-day."

And she left the nursery, and swung down-stairs on the rail of the banisters. But she did not go into the drawing-room; she opened the front door and went out into the moonshine.

It was a lovely night. But there was something strange about it. Everything looked asleep, and yet seemed not only awake but watching. There was not a sound, and yet the air seemed full of half-sounds. The child was quite alone, and yet at every step she fancied some one behind her, on one side of her, somewhere, and found it only a rustling leaf or a passing shadow. She was soon in the hayfield, where it was just the same; so that when she fancied that something green was moving near the first haycock she thought very little of it, till, coming closer, she plainly perceived by the moonlight a tiny man dressed in green, with a tall, pointed hat, and very, very long tips to his shoes, tying his shoestring with his foot on a stubble stalk. He had the most wizened of faces, and when he got angry with his shoe, he pulled so wry a grimace that it was quite laughable. At last he stood up, stepping carefully over the stubble, went up to the first haycock, and drawing out a hollow grass stalk blew upon it till his cheeks were puffed like footballs. And yet there was no sound, only a half-sound, as of a horn blown in the far distance, or in a dream. Presently the point of a tall hat, and finally just such another little wizened face, poked out through the side of the haycock.

"Can we hold revel here to-night?" asked the little green man.

"That indeed you cannot," answered the other; "we have hardly room to turn round as it is, with all Amelia's dirty frocks."

"Ah, bah!" said the dwarf; and he walked on to the next haycock, Amelia cautiously following.

Here he blew again, and a head was put out as before; on which he said,

"Can we hold revel here to-night?"

"How is it possible," was the reply, "when there is not a place where one can so much as set down an acorn cup, for Amelia's broken victuals?"

"Fie! fie!" said the dwarf, and went on to the third, where all happened as before; and he asked the old question,

"Can we hold revel here to-night?"

"Can you dance on glass and crockery sherds?" inquired the other. "Amelia's broken gimcracks are everywhere."

"Pshaw!" snorted the dwarf, frowning terribly; and when he came to the fourth haycock he blew such an angry blast that the grass stalk split into seven pieces. But he met with no better success than before. Only the point of a hat came through the hay, and a feeble voice piped in tones of depression—"The broken threads would entangle our feet. It's all Amelia's fault. If we could only get hold of her!"

"If she's wise, she'll keep as far from these haycocks as she can," snarled the dwarf, angrily; and he shook his fist as much as to say, "If she did come, I should not receive her very pleasantly."

Now with Amelia, to hear that she had better not do something, was to make her wish at once to do it; and as she was not at all wanting in courage, she pulled the dwarf's little cloak, just as she would have twitched her mother's shawl, and said (with that sort of snarly whine in which spoilt children generally speak)—"Why shouldn't I come to the haycocks if I want to? They belong to my papa, and I shall come if I like. But you have no business here."

"Nightshade and hemlock!" ejaculated the little man, "you are not lacking in impudence. Perhaps your Sauciness is not quite aware how things are distributed in this world?" saying which he lifted his pointed shoes and began to dance and sing,

"All under the sun belongs to men,
And all under the moon to the fairies.
So, so, so! Ho, ho, ho!
All under the moon to the fairies."

As he sang "Ho, ho, ho!" the little man turned head over heels; and though by this time Amelia would gladly have got away, she could not, for the dwarf seemed to dance and tumble round her, and always to cut off the chance of escape; whilst numberless voices from all around seemed to join in sthe chorus, with

"So, so, so! Ho, ho, ho!

All under the moon to the fairies."

"And now," said the little man, "to work! And you have plenty of work before you, so trip on, to the first haycock."

"I shan't!" said Amelia.

"On with you!" repeated the dwarf.

"I won't!" said Amelia.

But the little man, who was behind her, pinched her funny-bone with his lean fingers, and, as everybody knows, that is agony; so Amelia ran on, and tried to get away. But when she went too fast, the dwarf trod on her heels with his long-pointed shoe, and if she did not go fast enough, he pinched her funny-bone. So for once in her life she was obliged to do as she was told. As they ran, tall hats and wizened faces were popped out on all sides of the haycocks, like blanched almonds on a tipsy cake; and whenever the dwarf pinched Amelia, or trod on her heels, the goblins cried "Ho, ho, ho!" with such horrible contortions as they laughed, that it was hideous to behold them.

"Here is Amelia!" shouted the dwarf when they reached the first haycock.

"Ho, ho, ho!" laughed all the others, as they poked out here and there from the hay.

"Bring a stock," said the dwarf; on which the hay was lifted, and out ran six or seven dwarfs, carrying what seemed to Amelia to be a little girl like herself. And when she looked closer, to her horror and surprise the figure was exactly like her—it was her own face, clothes, and everything.

"Shall we kick it into the house?" asked the goblins.

"No," said the dwarf; "lay it down by the haycock. The father and mother are coming to seek her now."

When Amelia heard this she began to shriek for help; but she was pushed into the haycock, where her loudest cries sounded like the chirruping of a grasshopper.

It was really a fine sight to see the inside of the cock.

Farmers do not like to see flowers in a hayfield, but the fairies do. They had arranged all the buttercups, &c., in patterns on the haywalls; bunches of meadow-sweet swung from the roof like censers, and perfumed the air; and the ox-eye daisies which formed the ceiling gave a light like stars. But Amelia cared for none of this. She only struggled to peep through the hay, and she did see her father and mother and nurse come down the lawn, followed by the other servants, looking for her. When they saw the stock they ran to raise it with exclamations of pity and surprise. The stock moaned faintly, and Amelia's mamma wept, and Amelia herself shouted with all her might.

"What's that?" said her mamma. (It is not easy to deceive a mother.)

"Only the grasshoppers, my dear," said Papa. "Let us get the poor child home."

The stock moaned again, and the mother said, "Oh dear! oh dear-r-Ramelia!" and followed in tears.

"Rub her eyes," said the dwarf; on which Amelia's eyes were rubbed with some ointment, and when she took a last peep, she could see that the stock was nothing but a hairy imp, with a face like the oldest and most grotesque of apes.

"—and send her below," added the dwarf. On which the field opened, and Amelia was pushed underground.

She found herself on a sort of open heath, where no houses were to be seen. Of course there was no moonshine, and yet it was neither daylight nor dark. There was as the light of early dawn, and every sound was at once clear and dreamy, like the first sounds of the day coming through the fresh air before sunrise. Beautiful flowers crept over the heath, whose tints were constantly changing in the subdued light; and as the hues changed and blended, the flowers gave forth different perfumes. All would have been charming but that at every few paces the paths were blocked by large clothes-baskets full of dirty frocks, And the frocks were Amelia's. Torn, draggled, wet, covered with sand, mud, and dirt of all kinds, Amelia recognized them.

"You've got to wash them all," said the dwarf, who was behind her as usual; "that's what you've come down for—not because your society is particularly pleasant. So the sooner you begin the better."

"I can't," said Amelia (she had already learnt that "I won't" is not an answer for every one); "send them up to Nurse, and she'll do them. It is her business."

"What Nurse can do she has done, and now it's time for you to begin," said the dwarf. "Sooner or later the mischief done by spoilt children's wilful disobedience comes back on their own hands. Up to a certain point we help them, for we love children, and we are wilful ourselves. But there are limits to everything. If you can't wash your dirty frocks, it is time you learnt to do so, if only that you may know what the trouble is you impose on other people. *She* will teach you."

The dwarf kicked out his foot in front of him, and pointed with his long toe to a woman who sat by a fire made upon the heath, where a pot was suspended from crossed poles. It was like a bit of a gipsy encampment, and the woman seemed to be a real woman, not a fairy—which was the case, as Amelia afterwards found. She had lived underground for many years, and was the dwarfs' servant.

And this was how it came about that Amelia had to wash her dirty frocks. Let any little girl try to wash one of her dresses; not to half wash it, not to leave it stained with dirty water, but to wash it quite clean. Let her then try to starch and iron it—in short, to make it look as if it had come from the laundress—and she will have some idea of what poor Amelia had to learn to do. There was no help for it. When she was working she very seldom saw the dwarfs; but if she were idle or stubborn, or had any hopes of getting away, one was sure to start up at her elbow and pinch her funny-bone, or poke her in the ribs, till she did her best. Her back ached with stooping over the wash-tub; her hands and arms grew wrinkled with soaking in hot soapsuds, and sore with rubbing. Whatever she did not know how to do, the woman of the heath taught her. At first, whilst Amelia was sulky, the woman of the heath was sharp and cross; but when Amelia became willing and obedient, she was good-natured, and even helped her.

The first time that Amelia felt hungry she asked for some food.

"By all means," said one of the dwarfs; "there is plenty down here which belongs to you;" and he led her away till they came to a place like the first, except that it was covered with plates of broken meats; all the bits of good meat, pie, pudding, bread-and-butter, &c., that Amelia had wasted beforetime.

"I can't eat cold scraps like these," said Amelia, turning away.

"Then what did you ask for food for before you were hungry?" screamed the dwarf, and he pinched her and sent her about her business.

After a while she became so famished that she was glad to beg humbly to be allowed to go for food; and she ate a cold chop and the remains of a rice pudding with thankfulness. How delicious they tasted! She was surprised herself at the good things she had rejected. After a time she fancied she would like to warm up some of the cold meat in a pan, which the woman of the heath used to cook her own dinner in, and she asked for leave to do so.

"You may do anything you like to make yourself comfortable, if you do it yourself," said she; and Amelia, who had been watching her for many times, became quite expert in cooking up the scraps.

As there was no real daylight underground, so also there was no night. When the old woman was tired she lay down and had a nap, and when she thought that Amelia had earned a rest, she allowed her to do the same. It was never cold, and it never rained, so they slept on the heath among the flowers.

They say that "It's a long lane that has no turning," and the hardest tasks come to an end some time, and Amelia's dresses were clean at last; but then a more wearisome work was before her. They had to be mended. Amelia looked at the jagged rents made by the hedges; the great gaping holes in front where she had put her foot through; the torn tucks and gathers. First she wept, then she bitterly regretted that she had so often refused to do her sewing at home that she was very awkward with her needle. Whether she ever would have got through this task alone is doubtful, but she had by this time become so well-behaved and willing that the old woman was kind to her, and, pitying her blundering attempts, she helped her a great deal; whilst Amelia would cook the old woman's victuals, or repeat stories and pieces of poetry to amuse her.

"How glad I am that I ever learnt anything!" thought the poor child: "everything one learns seems to come in useful some time."

At last the dresses were finished.

"Do you think I shall be allowed to go home now?" Amelia asked of the woman of the heath.

"Not yet," said she; "you have got to mend the broken gimcracks next."

"But when I have done all my tasks," Amelia said; "will they let me go then?"

"That depends," said the woman, and she sat silent over the fire; but Amelia wept so bitterly, that she pitied her and said—"Only dry your eyes, for the fairies hate tears, and I will tell you all I know and do the best for you I can. You see, when you first came you were—excuse me!—such an unlicked cub; such a peevish, selfish, wilful, useless, and ill-mannered little miss, that neither the fairies nor anybody else were likely to keep you any longer than necessary. But now you are such a willing, handy, and civil little thing, and so pretty and graceful withal, that I think it is very likely that they will want to keep you altogether. I think you had better make up your mind to it. They are kindly little folk, and will make a pet of you in the end."

Juliana Horatia Ewing

"Oh, no! no!" moaned poor Amelia; "I want to be with my mother, my poor dear mother! I want to make up for being a bad child so long. Besides, surely that 'stock,' as they called her, will want to come back to her own people."

"As to that," said the woman, "after a time the stock will affect mortal illness, and will then take possession of the first black cat she sees, and in that shape leave the house, and come home. But the figure that is like you will remain lifeless in the bed, and will be duly buried. Then your people, believing you to be dead, will never look for you, and you will always remain here. However, as this distresses you so, I will give you some advice. Can you dance?"

"Yes," said Amelia; "I did attend pretty well to my dancing lessons. I was considered rather clever about it."

"At any spare moments you find," continued the woman, "dance, dance all your dances, and as well as you can. The dwarfs love dancing."

"And then?" said Amelia.

"Then, perhaps some night they will take you up to dance with them in the meadows above-ground."

"But I could not get away. They would tread on my heels—oh! I could never escape them."

"I know that," said the woman; "your only chance is this. If ever, when dancing in the meadows, you can find a four-leaved clover, hold it in your hand, and wish to be at home. Then no one can stop you. Meanwhile I advise you to seem happy, that they may think you are content, and have forgotten the world. And dance, above all, dance!"

And Amelia, not to be behindhand, began then and there to dance some pretty figures on the heath. As she was dancing the dwarf came by.

"Ho, ho!" said he, "you can dance, can you?"

"When I am happy I can," said Amelia, performing several graceful movements as she spoke.

"What are you pleased about now?" snapped the dwarf, suspiciously.

"Have I not reason?" said Amelia. "The dresses are washed and mended."

"Then up with them!" returned the dwarf. On which half-a-dozen elves popped the whole lot into a big basket and kicked them up into the world, where they found their way to the right wardrobes somehow.

As the woman of the heath had said, Amelia was soon set to a new task. When she bade the old woman farewell, she asked if she could do nothing for her if ever she got at liberty herself.

"Can I do nothing to get you back to your old home?" Amelia cried, for she thought of others now as well as herself.

"No, thank you," returned the old woman; "I am used to this, and do not care to return. I have been here a long time—how long I do not know; for as there is neither daylight nor dark we have no measure of time—long, I am sure, very long. The light and noise up yonder would now be too much for me. But I wish you well, and, above all, remember to dance!"

Juliana Horatia Ewing

The new scene of Amelia's labours was a more rocky part of the heath, where grey granite boulders served for seats and tables, and sometimes for workshops and anvils, as in one place, where a grotesque and grimy old dwarf sat forging rivets to mend china and glass. A fire in a hollow of the boulder served for a forge, and on the flatter part was his anvil. The rocks were covered in all directions with the knick-knacks, ornaments, &c., that Amelia had at various times destroyed.

"If you please, sir," she said to the dwarf, "I am Amelia."

The dwarf left off blowing at his forge and looked at her.

"Then I wonder you're not ashamed of yourself," said he.

"I am ashamed of myself," said poor Amelia, "very much ashamed. I should like to mend these things if I can."

"Well, you can't say more than that," said the dwarf, in a mollified tone, for he was a kindly little creature; "bring that china bowl here, and I'll show you how to set to work."

Poor Amelia did not get on very fast, but she tried her best. As to the dwarf, it was truly wonderful to see how he worked. Things seemed to mend themselves at his touch, and he was so proud of his skill, and so particular, that he generally did over again the things which Amelia had done after her fashion. The first time he gave her a few minutes in which to rest and amuse herself, she held out her little skirt, and began one of her prettiest dances.

"Rivets and trivets!" shrieked the little man, "how you dance! It is charming! I say it is charming! On with you! Fa, la fa! La, fa la! It gives me the fidgets in my shoe-points to see you!" and forthwith down he jumped, and began capering about.

"I am a good dancer myself," said the little man. "Do you know the 'Hop, Skip, and a Jump' dance?"

"I do not think I do," said Amelia.

"It is much admired," said the dwarf, "when I dance it;" and he thereupon tucked up the little leathern apron in which he worked, and performed some curious antics on one leg.

"That is the Hop," he observed, pausing for a moment. "The Skip is thus. You throw out your left leg as high and as far as you can, and as you drop on the toe of your left foot you fling out the right leg in the same manner, and so on. This is the Jump," with which he turned a somersault and disappeared from view. When Amelia next saw him he was sitting cross-legged on his boulder.

"Good, wasn't it?" he said.

"Wonderful!" Amelia replied.

"Now it's your turn again," said the dwarf.

But Amelia cunningly replied—"I'm afraid I must go on with my work."

"Pshaw!" said the little tinker. "Give me your work. I can do more in a minute than you in a month, and better to boot. Now dance again."

"Do you know this?" said Amelia, and she danced a few paces of a polka mazurka.

"Admirable!" cried the little man. "Stay"—and he drew an

old violin from behind the rock; "now dance again, and mark the time well, so that I may catch the measure, and then I will accompany you."

Which accordingly he did, improvising a very spirited tune, which had, however, the peculiar subdued and weird effect of all the other sounds in this strange region.

"The fiddle came from up yonder," said the little man. "It was smashed to atoms in the world and thrown away. But, ho, ho, ho! there is nothing that I cannot mend, and a mended fiddle is an amended fiddle. It improves the tone. Now teach me that dance, and I will patch up all the rest of the gimcracks. Is it a bargain?"

"By all means," said Amelia; and she began to explain the dance to the best of her ability.

"Charming, charming!" cried the dwarf. "We have no such dance ourselves. We only dance hand in hand, and round and round, when we dance together. Now I will learn the step, and then I will put my arm round your waist and dance with you."

Amelia looked at the dwarf. He was very smutty, and old, and wizened. Truly, a queer partner! But "handsome is that handsome does;" and he had done her a good turn. So when he had learnt the step, he put his arm round Amelia's waist, and they danced together. His shoe-points were very much in the way, but otherwise he danced very well.

Then he set to work on the broken ornaments, and they were all very soon "as good as new." But they were not kicked up into the world, for, as the dwarfs said, they would be sure to break on the road. So they kept them and used them; and I fear that no benefit came from the little tinker's skill to

Amelia's mamma's acquaintance in this matter.

"Have I any other tasks?" Amelia inquired.

"One more," said the dwarfs; and she was led farther on to a smooth mossy green, thickly covered with what looked like bits of broken thread. One would think it had been a milliner's work-room from the first invention of needles and thread.

"What are these?" Amelia asked.

"They are the broken threads of all the conversations you have interrupted," was the reply; "and pretty dangerous work it is to dance here now, with threads getting round one's shoe-points. Dance a hornpipe in a herring-net, and you'll know what it is!"

Amelia began to pick up the threads, but it was tedious work. She had cleared a yard or two, and her back was aching terribly, when she heard the fiddle and the mazurka behind her; and looking round she saw the old dwarf, who was playing away, and making the most hideous grimaces as his chin pressed the violin.

"Dance, my lady, dance!" he shouted.

"I do not think I can," said Amelia; "I am so weary with stooping over my work."

"Then rest a few minutes," he answered, "and I will play you a jig. A jig is a beautiful dance, such life, such spirit! So!"

And he played faster and faster, his arm, his face, his fiddle-bow all seemed working together; and as he played, the threads danced themselves into three heaps.

Juliana Horatia Ewing

"That is not bad, is it?" said the dwarf; "and now for our own dance," and he played the mazurka. "Get the measure well into your head. La, la fa la! la, la fa la! So!"

And throwing away his fiddle, he caught Amelia round the waist, and they danced as before. After which, she had no difficulty in putting the three heaps of thread into a basket.

"Where are these to be kicked to?" asked the young goblins.

"To the four winds of heaven," said the old dwarf. "There are very few drawing-room conversations worth putting together a second time. They are not like old china bowls."

BY MOONLIGHT

Thus Amelia's tasks were ended; but not a word was said of her return home. The dwarfs were now very kind, and made so much of her that it was evident that they meant her to remain with them. Amelia often cooked for them, and she danced and played with them, and never showed a sign of discontent; but her heart ached for home, and when she was alone she would bury her face in the flowers and cry for her mother.

One day she overheard the dwarfs in consultation.

"The moon is full to-morrow," said one—("Then I have been a month down here," thought Amelia; "it was full moon that night")—"shall we dance in the Mary Meads?"

"By all means," said the old tinker dwarf; "and we will take Amelia, and dance my dance."

"Is it safe?" said another.

"Look how content she is," said the old dwarf; "and, oh! how she dances; my feet tickle at the bare thought."

"The ordinary run of mortals do not see us," continued the objector; "but she is visible to any one. And there are men and women who wander in the moonlight, and the Mary Meads are near her old home."

"I will make her a hat of touchwood," said the old dwarf, "so that even if she is seen it will look like a will-o'-the-wisp bobbing up and down. If she does not come, I will not. I must dance my dance. You do not know what it is! We two alone move together with a grace which even here is remarkable. But when I think that up yonder we shall have attendant shadows echoing our movements, I long for the moment to arrive."

"So be it," said the others; and Amelia wore the touchwood hat, and went up with them to the Mary Meads.

Amelia and the dwarf danced the mazurka, and their shadows, now as short as themselves, then long and gigantic, danced beside them. As the moon went down, and the shadows lengthened, the dwarf was in raptures.

"When one sees how colossal one's very shadow is," he remarked, "one knows one's true worth. You also have a good shadow. We are partners in the dance, and I think we will be partners for life. But I have not fully considered the matter, so this is not to be regarded as a formal proposal." And he continued to dance, singing, "La, la, fa, la, la, la, fa, la." It was highly admired.

The Mary Meads lay a little below the house where Amelia's parents lived, and once during the night her father, who was watching by the sick bed of the stock, looked out of

Juliana Horatia Ewing

the window.

"How lovely the moonlight is!" he murmured; "but, dear me! there is a will-o'-the-wisp yonder. I had no idea the Mary Meads were so damp." Then he pulled the blind down and went back into the room.

As for poor Amelia, she found no four-leaved clover, and at cockcrow they all went underground.

"We will dance on Hunch Hill to-morrow," said the dwarfs.

All went as before; not a clover plant of any kind did Amelia see, and at cockcrow the revel broke up.

On the following night they danced in the hayfield. The old stubble was now almost hidden by green clover. There was a grand fairy dance—a round dance, which does not mean, as with us, a dance for two partners, but a dance where all join hands and dance round and round in a circle with appropriate antics. Round they went, faster and faster, the pointed shoes now meeting in the centre like the spokes of a wheel, now kicked out behind like spikes, and then scamper, caper, hurry! They seemed to fly, when suddenly the ring broke at one corner, and nothing being stronger than its weakest point, the whole circle were sent flying over the field.

"Ho, ho, ho!" laughed the dwarfs, for they are good-humoured little folk, and do not mind a tumble.

"Ha, ha, ha!" laughed Amelia, for she had fallen with her fingers on a four-leaved clover.

She put it behind her back, for the old tinker dwarf was coming up to her, wiping the mud from his face with his leathern apron.

"Now for our dance!" he shrieked. "And I have made up my mind—partners now and partners always. You are incomparable. For three hundred years I have not met with your equal."

But Amelia held the four-leaved clover above her head, and cried from her very heart—"I want to go home!"

The dwarf gave a hideous yell of disappointment, and at this instant the stock came tumbling head over heels into the midst, crying—"Oh! the pills, the powders, and the draughts! oh, the lotions and embrocations! oh, the blisters, the poultices, and the plasters! men may well be so short-lived!"

And Amelia found herself in bed in her own home.

AT HOME AGAIN

By the side of Amelia's bed stood a little table, on which were so many big bottles of medicine, that Amelia smiled to think of all the stock must have had to swallow during the month past. There was an open Bible on it too, in which Amelia's mother was reading, whilst tears trickled slowly down her pale cheeks. The poor lady looked so thin and ill, so worn with sorrow and watching, that Amelia's heart smote her, as if some one had given her a sharp blow.

"Mamma, Mamma! Mother, my dear, dear Mother!"

The tender, humble, loving tone of voice was so unlike Amelia's old imperious snarl, that her mother hardly recognized it; and when she saw Amelia's eyes full of intelligence instead of the delirium of fever, and that (though older and thinner and rather pale) she looked wonderfully well, the poor worn-out lady could hardly restrain herself from falling into hysterics for very joy.

"Dear Mamma, I want to tell you all about it," said Amelia, kissing the kind hand that stroked her brow.

But it appeared that the doctor had forbidden conversation; and though Amelia knew it would do her no harm, she yielded to her mother's wish and lay still and silent.

"Now, my love, it is time to take your medicine."

But Amelia pleaded—"Oh, Mamma, indeed I don't want any medicine. I am quite well, and would like to get up."

"Ah, my dear child!" cried her mother, "what I have suffered in inducing you to take your medicine, and yet see what good it has done you."

"I hope you will never suffer any more from my wilfulness," said Amelia; and she swallowed two tablespoonfuls of a mixture labelled "To be well shaken before taken," without even a wry face.

Presently the doctor came.

"You're not so very angry at the sight of me to-day, my little lady, eh?" he said.

"I have not seen you for a long time," said Amelia; "but I know you have been here, attending a stock who looked like me. If your eyes had been touched with fairy ointment, however, you would have been aware that it was a fairy imp, and a very ugly one, covered with hair. I have been living in terror lest it should go back underground in the shape of a black cat. However, thanks to the four-leaved clover, and the old woman of the heath, I am at home again."

On hearing this rhodomontade, Amelia's mother burst into tears, for she thought the poor child was still raving with fever. But the doctor smiled pleasantly, and said—"Ay, ay, to be sure," with a little nod, as one should say, "We know all about it;" and laid two fingers in a casual manner on Amelia's wrist.

"But she is wonderfully better, madam," he said afterwards to her mamma; "the brain has been severely tried, but she is marvellously improved: in fact, it is an effort of nature, a most favourable effort, and we can but assist the rally; we will change the medicine." Which he did, and very wisely assisted nature with a bottle of pure water flavoured with tincture of roses.

"And it was so very kind of him to give me his directions in poetry," said Amelia's mamma; "for I told him my memory, which is never good, seemed going completely, from anxiety, and if I had done anything wrong just now, I should never have forgiven myself. And I always found poetry easier to remember than prose,"—which puzzled everybody, the doctor included, till it appeared that she had ingeniously discovered a rhyme in his orders—

'To be kept cool and quiet,
With light nourishing diet.'

Under which treatment Amelia was soon pronounced to be well.

She made another attempt to relate her adventures, but she found that not even Nurse would believe in them.

"Why you told me yourself I might meet with the fairies," said Amelia, reproachfully.

"So I did, my dear," Nurse replied, "and they say that it's that put it into your head. And I'm sure what you say about the dwarfs and all is as good as a printed book, though you can't think that ever I would have let any dirty clothes store up like that, let alone your frocks, my dear. But for pity's sake, Miss Amelia, don't go on about it to your mother, for she thinks you'll never get your senses right again, and she has fretted enough about you, poor lady; and nursed you night and day till she is nigh worn out. And anybody can see you've been ill, Miss, you've grown so, and look paler and older like. Well, to be sure, as you say, if you'd been washing and working for a month in a place without a bit of sun, or a bed to lie on, and scraps to eat, it would be enough to do it; and many's the poor child that has to, and gets worn and old before her time. But, my dear, whatever you think, give in to your mother; you'll never repent giving in to your mother, my dear, the longest day you live."

So Amelia kept her own counsel. But she had one confidant.

When her parents brought the stock home on the night of Amelia's visit to the haycocks, the bulldog's conduct had been most strange. His usual good-humour appeared to have been exchanged for incomprehensible fury, and he was with difficulty prevented from flying at the stock, who on her part showed an anger and dislike fully equal to his.

Finally the bulldog had been confined to the stable, where he remained the whole month, uttering from time to time such howls, with his snub nose in the air, that poor Nurse quite gave up hope of Amelia's recovery.

"For indeed, my dear, they do say that a howling dog is a sign of death, and it was more than I could abear."

But the day after Amelia's return, as Nurse was leaving the

room with a tray which had carried some of the light nourishing diet ordered by the doctor, she was knocked down, tray and all, by the bulldog, who came tearing into the room, dragging a chain and dirty rope after him, and nearly choked by the desperate efforts which had finally effected his escape from the stable. And he jumped straight on to the end of Amelia's bed, where he lay, *thudding* with his tail, and giving short whines of ecstasy. And as Amelia begged that he might be left, and as it was evident that he would bite any one who tried to take him away, he became established as chief nurse. When Amelia's meals were brought to the bedside on a tray, he kept a fixed eye on the plates, as if to see if her appetite were improving. And he would even take a snack himself, with an air of great affability.

And when Amelia told him her story, she could see by his eyes, and his nose, and his ears, and his tail, and the way he growled whenever the stock was mentioned, that he knew all about it. As, on the other hand, he had no difficulty in conveying to her by sympathetic whines the sentiment, "Of course I would have helped you if I could; but they tied me up, and this disgusting old rope has taken me a month to worry through."

So, in spite of the past, Amelia grew up good and gentle, unselfish and considerate for others. She was unusually clever, as those who have been with the "Little People" are said always to be.

And she became so popular with her mother's acquaintances that they said—"We will no longer call her Amelia, for it is a name we learnt to dislike, but we will call her Amy, that is to say, 'Beloved.'"

* * * * *

Juliana Horatia Ewing

"And did my godmother's grandmother believe that Amelia had really been with the fairies, or did she think it was all fever ravings?"

"That, indeed, she never said, but she always observed that it was a pleasant tale with a good moral, which was surely enough for anybody."

THE END

ABOUT THE AUTHOR

 **Mrs. Juliana Horatia Ewing** (née Gatty) (1841–1885) was a writer of children's stories, daughter of The Rev. Alfred Gatty and Margaret Gatty, also a writer for children. Among her tales, which have hardly been excelled in sympathetic insight into child-life, and still enjoy undiminished popularity, are: Mrs. Overtheway's Remembrances (1869), A Flat Iron for a Farthing (1872), Six to Sixteen (1875), Jan of the Windmill (1876), Jackanapes (1884), and The Story of a Short Life (1885).

Her works have been called the "first outstanding child-novels" in English literature.[1]

She was born at Ecclesfield, Yorkshire on August 3, 1841; married June 1, 1867, to Alexander Ewing and died at Bath, May 13, 1885. She was buried at Trull, Somerset, on May 16, 1885.

Other books by this author

A Flat Iron for a Farthing

A Great Emergency and Other Tales

Jan of the Windmill

Melchior's Dream and Other Tales

Miscellanea

Mrs. Overtheway's Remembrances

Brothers of Pity and Other Tales of Beasts and Men

Choose from Thousands of 1stWorldLibrary Classics By

A. M. Barnard
Ada Leverson
Adolphus William Ward
Aesop
Agatha Christie
Alexander Aaronsohn
Alexander Kielland
Alexandre Dumas
Alfred Gatty
Alfred Ollivant
Alice Duer Miller
Alice Turner Curtis
Alice Dunbar
Allen Chapman
Alleyne Ireland
Ambrose Bierce
Amelia E. Barr
Amory H. Bradford
Andrew Lang
Andrew McFarland Davis
Andy Adams
Angela Brazil
Anna Alice Chapin
Anna Sewell
Annie Besant
Annie Hamilton Donnell
Annie Payson Call
Annie Roe Carr
Annonaymous
Anton Chekhov
Archibald Lee Fletcher
Arnold Bennett
Arthur C. Benson
Arthur Conan Doyle
Arthur M. Winfield
Arthur Ransome
Arthur Schnitzler
Arthur Train
Atticus
B.H. Baden-Powell
B. M. Bower
B. C. Chatterjee
Baroness Emmuska Orczy
Baroness Orczy
Basil King
Bayard Taylor
Ben Macomber
Bertha Muzzy Bower
Bjornstjerne Bjornson

Booth Tarkington
Boyd Cable
Bram Stoker
C. Collodi
C. E. Orr
C. M. Ingleby
Carolyn Wells
Catherine Parr Traill
Charles A. Eastman
Charles Amory Beach
Charles Dickens
Charles Dudley Warner
Charles Farrar Browne
Charles Ives
Charles Kingsley
Charles Klein
Charles Hanson Towne
Charles Lathrop Pack
Charles Romyn Dake
Charles Whibley
Charles Willing Beale
Charlotte M. Braeme
Charlotte M. Yonge
Charlotte Perkins Stetson
Clair W. Hayes
Clarence Day Jr.
Clarence E. Mulford
Clemence Housman
Confucius
Coningsby Dawson
Cornelis DeWitt Wilcox
Cyril Burleigh
D. H. Lawrence
Daniel Defoe
David Garnett
Dinah Craik
Don Carlos Janes
Donald Keyhoe
Dorothy Kilner
Dougan Clark
Douglas Fairbanks
E. Nesbit
E. P. Roe
E. Phillips Oppenheim
E. S. Brooks
Earl Barnes
Edgar Rice Burroughs
Edith Van Dyne
Edith Wharton

Edward Everett Hale
Edward J. O'Biren
Edward S. Ellis
Edwin L. Arnold
Eleanor Atkins
Eleanor Hallowell Abbott
Eliot Gregory
Elizabeth Gaskell
Elizabeth McCracken
Elizabeth Von Arnim
Ellem Key
Emerson Hough
Emilie F. Carlen
Emily Bronte
Emily Dickinson
Enid Bagnold
Enilor Macartney Lane
Erasmus W. Jones
Ernie Howard Pie
Ethel May Dell
Ethel Turner
Ethel Watts Mumford
Eugene Sue
Eugenie Foa
Eugene Wood
Eustace Hale Ball
Evelyn Everett-green
Everard Cotes
F. H. Cheley
F. J. Cross
F. Marion Crawford
Fannie E. Newberry
Federick Austin Ogg
Ferdinand Ossendowski
Fergus Hume
Florence A. Kilpatrick
Fremont B. Deering
Francis Bacon
Francis Darwin
Frances Hodgson Burnett
Frances Parkinson Keyes
Frank Gee Patchin
Frank Harris
Frank Jewett Mather
Frank L. Packard
Frank V. Webster
Frederic Stewart Isham
Frederick Trevor Hill
Frederick Winslow Taylor

Friedrich Kerst
Friedrich Nietzsche
Fyodor Dostoyevsky
G.A. Henty
G.K. Chesterton
Gabrielle E. Jackson
Garrett P. Serviss
Gaston Leroux
George A. Warren
George Ade
Geroge Bernard Shaw
George Cary Eggleston
George Durston
George Ebers
George Eliot
George Gissing
George MacDonald
George Meredith
George Orwell
George Sylvester Viereck
George Tucker
George W. Cable
George Wharton James
Gertrude Atherton
Gordon Casserly
Grace E. King
Grace Gallatin
Grace Greenwood
Grant Allen
Guillermo A. Sherwell
Gulielma Zollinger
Gustav Flaubert
H. A. Cody
H. B. Irving
H. C. Bailey
H. G. Wells
H. H. Munro
H. Irving Hancock
H. R. Naylor
H. Rider Haggard
H. W. C. Davis
Haldeman Julius
Hall Caine
Hamilton Wright Mabie
Hans Christian Andersen
Harold Avery
Harold McGrath
Harriet Beecher Stowe
Harry Castlemon
Harry Coghill
Harry Houidini

Hayden Carruth
Helent Hunt Jackson
Helen Nicolay
Hendrik Conscience
Hendy David Thoreau
Henri Barbusse
Henrik Ibsen
Henry Adams
Henry Ford
Henry Frost
Henry James
Henry Jones Ford
Henry Seton Merriman
Henry W Longfellow
Herbert A. Giles
Herbert Carter
Herbert N. Casson
Herman Hesse
Hildegard G. Frey
Homer
Honore De Balzac
Horace B. Day
Horace Walpole
Horatio Alger Jr.
Howard Pyle
Howard R. Garis
Hugh Lofting
Hugh Walpole
Humphry Ward
Ian Maclaren
Inez Haynes Gillmore
Irving Bacheller
Isabel Cecilia Williams
Isabel Hornibrook
Israel Abrahams
Ivan Turgenev
J. G.Austin
J. Henri Fabre
J. M. Barrie
J. M. Walsh
J. Macdonald Oxley
J. R. Miller
J. S. Fletcher
J. S. Knowles
J. Storer Clouston
J. W. Duffield
Jack London
Jacob Abbott
James Allen
James Andrews
James Baldwin

James Branch Cabell
James DeMille
James Joyce
James Lane Allen
James Lane Allen
James Oliver Curwood
James Oppenheim
James Otis
James R. Driscoll
Jane Abbott
Jane Austen
Jane L. Stewart
Janet Aldridge
Jens Peter Jacobsen
Jerome K. Jerome
Jessie Graham Flower
John Buchan
John Burroughs
John Cournos
John F. Kennedy
John Gay
John Glasworthy
John Habberton
John Joy Bell
John Kendrick Bangs
John Milton
John Philip Sousa
John Taintor Foote
Jonas Lauritz Idemil Lie
Jonathan Swift
Joseph A. Altsheler
Joseph Carey
Joseph Conrad
Joseph E. Badger Jr
Joseph Hergesheimer
Joseph Jacobs
Jules Vernes
Julian Hawthrone
Julie A Lippmann
Justin Huntly McCarthy
Kakuzo Okakura
Karle Wilson Baker
Kate Chopin
Kenneth Grahame
Kenneth McGaffey
Kate Langley Bosher
Kate Langley Bosher
Katherine Cecil Thurston
Katherine Stokes
L. A. Abbot
L. T. Meade

L. Frank Baum
Latta Griswold
Laura Dent Crane
Laura Lee Hope
Laurence Housman
Lawrence Beasley
Leo Tolstoy
Leonid Andreyev
Lewis Carroll
Lewis Sperry Chafer
Lilian Bell
Lloyd Osbourne
Louis Hughes
Louis Joseph Vance
Louis Tracy
Louisa May Alcott
Lucy Fitch Perkins
Lucy Maud Montgomery
Luther Benson
Lydia Miller Middleton
Lyndon Orr
M. Corvus
M. H. Adams
Margaret E. Sangster
Margret Howth
Margaret Vandercook
Margaret W. Hungerford
Margret Penrose
Maria Edgeworth
Maria Thompson Daviess
Mariano Azuela
Marion Polk Angellotti
Mark Overton
Mark Twain
Mary Austin
Mary Catherine Crowley
Mary Cole
Mary Hastings Bradley
Mary Roberts Rinehart
Mary Rowlandson
M. Wollstonecraft Shelley
Maud Lindsay
Max Beerbohm
Myra Kelly
Nathaniel Hawthrone
Nicolo Machiavelli
O. F. Walton
Oscar Wilde
Owen Johnson
P.G. Wodehouse
Paul and Mabel Thorne

Paul G. Tomlinson
Paul Severing
Percy Brebner
Percy Keese Fitzhugh
Peter B. Kyne
Plato
Quincy Allen
R. Derby Holmes
R. L. Stevenson
R. S. Ball
Rabindranath Tagore
Rahul Alvares
Ralph Bonehill
Ralph Henry Barbour
Ralph Victor
Ralph Waldo Emmerson
Rene Descartes
Ray Cummings
Rex Beach
Rex E. Beach
Richard Harding Davis
Richard Jefferies
Richard Le Gallienne
Robert Barr
Robert Frost
Robert Gordon Anderson
Robert L. Drake
Robert Lansing
Robert Lynd
Robert Michael Ballantyne
Robert W. Chambers
Rosa Nouchette Carey
Rudyard Kipling
Saint Augustine
Samuel B. Allison
Samuel Hopkins Adams
Sarah Bernhardt
Sarah C. Hallowell
Selma Lagerlof
Sherwood Anderson
Sigmund Freud
Standish O'Grady
Stanley Weyman
Stella Benson
Stella M. Francis
Stephen Crane
Stewart Edward White
Stijn Streuvels
Swami Abhedananda
Swami Parmananda
T. S. Ackland

T. S. Arthur
The Princess Der Ling
Thomas A. Janvier
Thomas A Kempis
Thomas Anderton
Thomas Bailey Aldrich
Thomas Bulfinch
Thomas De Quincey
Thomas Dixon
Thomas H. Huxley
Thomas Hardy
Thomas More
Thornton W. Burgess
U. S. Grant
Upton Sinclair
Valentine Williams
Various Authors
Vaughan Kester
Victor Appleton
Victor G. Durham
Victoria Cross
Virginia Woolf
Wadsworth Camp
Walter Camp
Walter Scott
Washington Irving
Wilbur Lawton
Wilkie Collins
Willa Cather
Willard F. Baker
William Dean Howells
William le Queux
W. Makepeace Thackeray
William W. Walter
William Shakespeare
Winston Churchill
Yei Theodora Ozaki
Yogi Ramacharaka
Young E. Allison
Zane Grey